SUNKEN SEAS

A ROWAN GRAY MYSTERY BOOK FOUR

LILY HARPER HART

HARPERHART PUBLICATIONS

Copyright © 2017 by Lily Harper Hart

All rights reserved.

No part of this book may be reproduced in any form or by any electronic or mechanical means, including information storage and retrieval systems, without written permission from the author, except for the use of brief quotations in a book review.

❦ Created with Vellum

ONE

"Again? You're going to kill me, woman."

Rowan Gray looked up from the sandcastle she toiled over and fixed her boyfriend Quinn Davenport with a mischievous smile as he offered up a mock growl and joined her on the beachy expanse.

It was early in the day, the sun low in the sky and the heat far from blistering, and Rowan was happy to have some quiet time. Since she worked on a cruise ship – something that was a relatively new experience – she'd found that she enjoyed her down time far more than she used to when she worked as a photographer for a Detroit newspaper.

"Did you find my note?"

Quinn, his short hair fresh from a shower, offered up a rueful grin. "The rather elaborate note that told me exactly where you were going to be and what you were going to be doing? The one you put on the pillow next to my head so I wouldn't wake alone? Yeah, I found it."

Rowan's stomach did a little jig at his playful expression. They'd only been dating a couple weeks – finally taking the plunge and spending "clothing optional" nights together after a rather tense and sexually heightened stretch – and they were in that heady new part of the relationship that often left them both breathless and excited whenever they were in close proximity to one another. "You could've just said you were on the beach. I particularly liked the little sketch you did of what you would look like on the beach so I would be sure to recognize you."

Rowan was sheepish. "Sorry. I couldn't sleep."

"You should've woken me." Quinn snagged Rowan's hand and gave it a squeeze as she worked on her project. "You didn't have to come out here and build a sandcastle to distract yourself from the temptation of my naked body."

Rowan blinked several times in rapid succession as his words slipped into place. "You're kind of full of yourself."

Quinn bobbed his head. "I am."

"It's kind of cute."

"That's what I was going for." Quinn leaned forward and pressed a soft kiss to the corner of Rowan's mouth. Before her arrival on The Bounding Storm, the ship where he served as security chief, he fancied himself a footloose and fancy-free bachelor for the immediate future ... if not forever. From the moment she arrived, though, he was drawn to her. He couldn't explain it and, ultimately, he couldn't fight it. He wasn't much of a relationship guy before Rowan hit the ship, but now he couldn't imagine how he made it before her ... and they'd only been together for a few weeks. It was altogether frightening and exciting at the same time.

"What are you thinking about?" Rowan asked curiously, catching the shift in his demeanor as she worked on a turret.

"You." Quinn saw no reason to lie. "I seem to think about you a lot these days."

Rowan's cheeks burned as she focused on the castle. She was afraid if she met his steady gaze that she would end up ripping his clothes off with her teeth as they played at plundering the castle. "Oh. That's sweet."

"No, what's sweet is how red your face gets when you're embarrassed."

Rowan pursed her lips. "I wasn't embarrassed."

"Yes, you were."

"Was not."

"Was, too."

Rather than let the conversation devolve into something that would require a lot of energy, Rowan merely shrugged. "Fine. Maybe I was embarrassed. I still think it's a sweet sentiment."

"I can live with that." Quinn shifted so he was closer to Rowan, their knees touching as they sat cross-legged. "How come you always want to build a sandcastle when we're at port?"

"Honestly?"

Quinn nodded.

"I find it relaxing," Rowan replied. "I'm not sure how to explain it. "I like the sound of the ocean, the breeze in my hair. I like the sun before it gets too hot. I like the way the cool sand, the sand underneath the top stuff, feels when I'm working with it. It's weird but ... it's kind of like meditating or something."

"I don't think it's that weird," Quinn countered. "I think it's fairly sweet and cute." He dug in the sand and came up with a handful of damp mud. "I was thinking I might build the castle's official garage."

Rowan giggled, amused. "You could do that."

"Cool." Quinn set to work. He wasn't yet familiar with all of Rowan's moods – although he was getting there – and he was certain something else was behind her need to build a sandcastle whenever they hit port.

The first several times she did it he thought it was absolutely adorable. It wasn't until the third time he started noticing a pattern. By the fifth time, he could track her moods by the castle she built. He was both fascinated and troubled by the phenomenon.

"Did you spend a lot of time at the beach when you were a kid?" Quinn asked after several minutes of silence.

Rowan shrugged. "We spent a lot of time by lakes. We had a

cottage in the Thumb – that's the Michigan thumb – and we spent most of our summers there before ... well, before my mother died."

Quinn nodded. He knew Rowan remained troubled by her mother's death even though she was barely into her teen years when it happened. Worse than her mother's death, though, was the disappearance of her father when she was eighteen. Rowan could grasp that her mother was gone and didn't leave of her own volition. What happened to Rowan's father – the only parent she had remaining – was a mystery. Did he pick up and leave on his own? Was he dead? Did something else happen to him? These were the questions that plagued Rowan even though she was determined to put everything behind her. Quinn wanted to help her find answers, but he had no idea where to start.

"Did you make sandcastles on Michigan beaches?" Quinn asked.

"I did." Rowan smiled at the memory. "My mother used to help me. We'd make these huge castles." She held her arms up and out for emphasis. "They were extremely elaborate. My father thought it was a waste of time and yet he always took photographs of them. I have an entire collection of sandcastle photos from when I was younger."

"I would like to see them."

Rowan snorted, genuinely amused. "Why?"

Quinn opted for honesty. "Because they're important to you. That means they're important to me."

Rowan's heart melted. If she wasn't already desperately smitten, that would've tipped her right over the edge. "How come you always know the right thing to say?"

"I think that's only your perception," Quinn said dryly. "If you ask my mother – heck, if you ask anyone else in my family – they'll tell you I'm a 'speak first and think about it second' type of person."

Rowan smiled, the expression lighting up her pretty face. Quinn loved watching her on the mornings when she chose to hit the beach. The way the sun set off her auburn hair made him think of a wildfire.

"I still think you always know the right thing to say to me," Rowan pressed.

"Maybe you bring it out of me." Quinn gripped Rowan's hand and took her by surprise when he pressed a kiss to her knuckles. It was a schmaltzy and yet heartfelt moment and she knew she would remember it for a very long time. "I'm just trying to understand why you like building sandcastles. I enjoy it. I think it's fun. You seem to need to do it, though."

"I told you. It relaxes me."

"There's something more." Quinn knit his eyebrows as he tried to draw the answer out of her. Finally, he gave up. "When you're ready, you'll tell me."

Rowan balked. "I just like building them and think it's relaxing."

Quinn tilted his head to the side, considering. "Maybe you don't even understand why you're doing it. I guess we'll have to discover that together."

Rowan had no idea how to respond to that so she merely shrugged. "I guess." Desperate to change the subject, she glommed on to their upcoming trip. "So, what can you tell me about this treasure-seeking group we're going to be taking on?"

Quinn knew exactly what she was doing – and why – but he opted not to call her on it. She didn't want to be pushed and he understood the inclination to keep certain things to herself. He could wait her out on the sandcastles, and he'd learned his lesson several times over when it came to pushing her.

"I don't know if I'd call them treasure seekers," Quinn hedged. "You probably shouldn't say that in front of them."

"I'm sure I can refrain," Rowan said so dryly Quinn could do nothing but laugh.

"It's a big deal," Quinn said after a beat. "The Conqueror was originally supposed to travel between Europe and Florida during the Revolutionary War. It had additional troops – although nowhere near what people thought the Americans needed to win – and it had money stored on it."

"Do you know much about the history?"

Quinn shrugged. He was something of a history buff but wanted to remain "cool" in Rowan's eyes so he worked overtime to tamp down his enthusiasm. "I read up about it when I heard they were coming."

Rowan stared at him for several moments, internally debating how she should respond. Finally, she could do nothing but laugh. "I saw the history books in your cabin long before this trip came about. I know you're a history geek."

Quinn scowled. "I don't like the word 'geek.'"

"I'm sorry." Rowan was instantly contrite. "I know you're a history stud. Please continue."

"That's better." Quinn attempted to remain stern but lost the battle when he saw the way Rowan's lips curved. "You think you're funny, don't you?"

"I think you always make me smile these days and I'm grateful."

The heartfelt declaration was enough to cause Quinn's heart to stutter – something he wasn't prepared for – and he merely shook his head to dislodge the lovey-dovey thoughts invading his brain. "You steal the breath from me sometimes."

"Right back at you."

Quinn grinned as he regrouped. "Anyway ... what was I saying?"

"You were being a history stud and telling me about The Conqueror."

"Oh, right." Even though part of him was in the mood to be romantic, Quinn was happy to share his ship knowledge. He figured he could romance Rowan as soon as she was done with her castle, which left him plenty of time to talk about what he considered to be one of the greatest ship finds ... well, ever.

"So, The Conqueror set sail from Portugal in 1777. It was supposed to take several months to arrive. The men on board were mercenaries rather than troops, but I believe the rationale for sending them was that it would be impossible for the Americans to win, so why not send people they didn't care about surviving for the cause."

Rowan made a face. "That's ... delightful."

"Well, it happened a long time ago, so don't get worked up."

"Yeah, yeah."

Quinn smirked. "Anyway, like I said, the ship never arrived. It was believed to have sunk in the middle of the ocean, someplace it would be lost for all time. Two months ago, though, divers filming one of those documentaries for *Shark Week* happened upon something they couldn't explain.

"When they got closer for inspection – and that took some time because they had to bring in more heavy duty equipment – they found a handful of coins and a desk plate," he continued. "They also found a reef that looked suspiciously like the remnants of a ship.

"The area has been cordoned off for two months while the coins and plate were researched, but about a week ago information came back," he continued. "The coins were Portuguese in origin ... and the desk plate belonged to the captain of The Conqueror."

Rowan furrowed her brow. "And it was found where again?"

"Between Miami and the Bahamas. There's a small island out there – very small, by the way – and we'll be docking there."

"What's it called?"

"El Demonio."

"Isn't that Spanish for demon?"

Quinn nodded.

"So we're going to Demon Island?"

"I guess. I never really thought about it." Quinn's grin was impish. "Does that frighten you? If so, I think I can arrange it so you won't be alone when you go to sleep during the trip. In fact, I know the perfect guy to act as your bodyguard."

Even though she was interested in hearing more, Rowan couldn't stop herself from smiling. "Is that so?"

"Yes."

"We'll negotiate terms on that later," Rowan said. "For now, go back to The Conqueror. How is this going to work? I mean, I know we have a lot of historians and professional divers hitting the ship tomorrow, but I'm not sure what to expect once they get here."

In truth, Quinn wasn't sure what to expect either. "My understanding is that everyone will start arriving in the morning. It's not going to be a full load, but the excavation company in charge bought out the entire ship. It's more like a quarter load when you add up everyone."

"But they all won't be diving, right?"

Quinn shook his head. "The dive team is relatively small. I believe the primary team, those with the most clearance, is only about twenty people. The extended team is about a hundred people. They'll oversee setting their own schedule so we'll just have to watch and get vicarious thrills through them."

"And the other people?"

"They've got people trained to clean whatever treasure they find. They've got map experts, ship experts, and a bunch of historians. This could be a huge find."

"And you're excited because you're a history geek."

Quinn extended a warning finger. "Stud. I'm a history stud."

"You're definitely a stud. I ... ." Rowan didn't get a chance to finish what she was going to say because Quinn picked that moment to tackle her into the sand, rolling her so his body was on top and she was pinned between him and the ground. "Well, I see you're about to demonstrate your stud factor," she said when she caught her breath.

Quinn's smile was so wide it almost swallowed his entire face as he leaned over. His lips were mere inches from hers and he was desperate to press them together. He wasn't done playing yet, though.

"Have I ever told you about my dreams of being a professional swashbuckler when I was a kid?"

The question caught Rowan off guard. "I don't believe so."

"When I was a young man – still a stud, mind you – I didn't know a swashbuckler wasn't a real thing. I thought it was just another form of pirate ... but a good pirate who gets the girl and doesn't do anything illegal."

Rowan snorted. "You were a rule follower even as a kid, weren't you?"

Quinn shrugged, unbothered by the challenge in her voice. "I like a bit of order to my day. That's why I joined the military. Sue me."

"No. I like a little order in my day, too. That's why we get along so well. I especially like it when you decide to organize everything – including your socks – and go on a mission to make sure they're all paired before we go to sleep."

"Ha, ha." Quinn wrinkled his nose. "I like things a certain way. I'm not going to deny it."

"I like things a certain way, too," Rowan admitted. "I like them this way." She planted her dirty hands on either side of Quinn's face and then raised her head so she could smack her lips against his. "I like this a lot."

Even though he wanted to be in charge of the game, Quinn couldn't stop himself from smiling. She was far too appealing to restrain for long periods of time. "I like this a lot, too. I was in the middle of a story, though."

Rowan was contrite. "I'm sorry. Continue with your swashbuckling story."

"I always wanted to find hidden treasure," Quinn explained. "You know the movie *The Goonies*? That's my idea of perfection."

Rowan smiled at the admission. "I absolutely love that movie. I wanted so badly to go on an adventure during rainy days when I was a kid. It never happened, but that didn't stop me from dreaming."

"I wanted that, too. The thing is, we're about to do it as adults. It's not exactly the same, but it's not altogether different either."

"And you're excited about it." Rowan's eyes sparkled. "You're so excited about this you're ready to burst."

"I'm excited about a lot of things," Quinn clarified. "I am excited about this, though. I'm also excited because we get to share it together."

"So we get to be swashbucklers together?" Rowan was trying to tease him, but he was so earnest she couldn't help but join in his enthusiasm. "Do you have books you can show me so I can learn something about The Conqueror, too?"

"Oh, now I think you're trying to placate me." Quinn poked her side. "You don't like history books. You don't have to pretend."

"Honestly? It's not that I don't like history books. I could take them or leave them. I simply don't care. You, though, you care. You get all fired up. I think that if we look at history books together and then ... um, play another sort of swashbuckling game ... it might work out to my advantage."

Quinn was tickled by her playful attitude. "I'm open to finding out."

"That goes for both of us."

He lowered his mouth and pressed his lips to hers, the exchange soft and full of promise. "We need to hit a few stores before then, though. I need to do some shopping before we leave port."

"Okay."

"How about we make a day of it?" Quinn suggested, warming to the idea. "We can shop. Then I'll take you to a nice dinner, something full of romance and candles. Then, when we get back to the ship, I'll clobber you over the head with history and then ravish you like a proper pirate."

Rowan couldn't hide her delight. "Can we fit ice cream in there, too?"

"Absolutely."

"Then that sounds like the perfect day."

"That's exactly what I was going for."

TWO

Rowan and Quinn's afternoon of shopping turned into a delightful date.

Rowan amused herself watching Quinn as he pored through possibilities in the bookstore. Quinn was happy to watch Rowan try on three different dresses – and make his opinion known when she finally selected one.

They looked at new boat shoes for Quinn, new earrings for Rowan, and even spent a decent amount of time in an art gallery simply browsing because they both enjoyed the bright colors and nautical themes.

By the time dinner rolled around, they were both starving and ready to put an end to their day so they could return to the ship and start swashbuckling.

"This place looks nice," Rowan noted as they passed a restaurant that had an expansive outdoor section. "They have open tables right on the water."

Quinn stopped at the front of the restaurant to peruse the menu. "And they have lobster and crab legs on special tonight. I happen to know how you feel about crab legs so I think this is a good choice."

Rowan arched a dubious eyebrow. "And how do I feel about crab legs?"

"Ro, if you could find a way to have sex with the crab legs instead of me, you would totally do it."

"Uh-uh." Rowan emphatically shook her head. "You would definitely win out over crab legs."

"Oh, you're so sweet."

"If I could find a way to combine you with crab legs, though, I would never leave my cabin again."

Quinn barked out a laugh as he held open the door and ushered Rowan inside. "Now that right there sounds like an experiment we should both get down with."

The hostess was young and pretty, her eyes lighting up when she caught sight of Quinn. She tucked a strand of her dark hair behind her ear as he asked for an outdoor table, barely sparing Rowan a glance as they shuffled through the restaurant interior before hitting the waterfront.

"Will this do?" The hostess gestured toward a table that had a perfect view of the ocean.

"This is great." Quinn smiled at her, although the expression was remote, and pulled out Rowan's chair. "It's romantic and everything. Thank you."

The hostess stilled. "Romantic? Oh, *right*." She cast Rowan an unreadable look. "Well, have fun with your romance." She seemed to lose interest quickly as she put the menus in Quinn's hands and hurried back to the front of the restaurant.

Rowan chuckled as Quinn got settled across from her. "You have a very strange effect on women."

"Oh, yeah? What's that?"

"They all want to jump you within seconds of meeting you."

"I guess I just have one of those faces."

"And bodies."

Quinn pursed his lips. "Did you want to jump me within seconds of meeting me?"

The question was direct and Rowan was glad the outdoor ambiance was dark so Quinn wouldn't be able to see her cheeks heating up. "Of course not."

"Lies." Quinn smirked. "I think you felt exactly what I did when I saw you for the first time."

"Which was?"

"I kept thinking there had to be a way for me to get you naked without getting involved in a relationship." Quinn refused to lie. "I was terrified to get involved with you."

"How come?"

"Because I wasn't in the mood to get attached to anyone. I was in the middle of a brooding session – one that seemed to last for years – and I kind of liked the idea of being the ship loner. Women hit on me all the time – and I do mean *all* the time – but I turned them down."

Rowan frowned. "I don't need to hear how many people hit on you."

"Come on. It's fun for both of us."

Rowan rolled her eyes. "Your ego is out of control."

"That's one of the things you like best about me," Quinn teased, easing back in his chair and extending his legs in front of him. "I was determined not to get involved with you and yet that only lasted for two days. I swear it's true. Somehow, within two days, you had me completely rethinking my strategy. I think you must be magic."

Rowan was chagrined. Technically she was magic, at least in a roundabout way. It was something she'd become more comfortable talking about – at least with Quinn – but she remained uneasy with other people.

Ever since she became interested in taking photographs as a youngster she'd been able to do something a bit odd. It wasn't the camera. It wasn't the film – which she obviously no longer used, although she did when she first started. It was her. Ultimately she deduced it didn't matter which camera she utilized, when she snapped photographs a certain death omen popped up warning her when people were in danger of losing their lives.

Rowan was in the middle of her first shift on The Bounding Storm when the problem reared its ugly head. She thought she wouldn't have to worry about it on a cruise ship – that was supposed to be a happy and safe place, after all – but she'd been wrong. She'd reluctantly told Quinn the truth, and instead of thinking she was crazy, he opted to help.

That started a slow burn that neither of them could fight and within a short amount of time Quinn was ready to try a relationship. His busy mind wouldn't relent until he embraced the idea. Rowan was more reluctant, convinced he would change his mind after getting to know her. He hadn't, though. They were still together weeks later and their relationship had only grown stronger.

Sure, the death omen had popped up a few more times, but they dealt with it together when it became an issue and Rowan was slowly coming to the realization that her relationship with Quinn wasn't necessarily doomed from the start. That filled her with a different kind of anxiety – one she couldn't possibly share with him – but she was genuinely happy with their status as The Bounding Storm's new "it" couple.

Of course, the bulk of the female staff on the ship weren't happy because Quinn was considered quite the catch, but Rowan wasn't the type to feel guilty ... especially because she was completely happy reveling in her victory.

Quinn snapped his fingers in front of Rowan's face to get her attention. "Where did you just go?"

Rowan's already red cheeks burned hotter. "I ... was just thinking."

"About what?"

Rowan sipped her water and swallowed hard. She decided not to avert or brush off the question. "How happy I am. I wasn't sure it was possible for me because ... well, just because ... but apparently it is."

Quinn's smile was slow and deliberate. "Yeah, we definitely need to stuff your face with crab legs and then get out of here. I have some very definite plans for us tonight."

Rowan snorted as she turned her full attention to her menu. "So I'm going to eat crab legs, you're going to geek out with your new book, and then we're going to swashbuckle each other. That sounds like a fun evening."

"I think it will be one for the history books."

QUINN AND ROWAN PLACED their orders and turned the conversation back to The Conqueror. Rowan was legitimately curious and Quinn was like a kid who discovered his favorite superhero movie was actually good. He couldn't get enough of talking about the ship.

"So they wouldn't have had any life rafts or anything to save the crew?" Rowan asked.

Quinn shook his head as he sipped his beer. "No. Back in those days, there was no point. If a big ship couldn't make it to its destination, there was no way a little ship could. It would've simply been delaying the inevitable."

"That's kind of sad." Rowan played with the condensation ring her piña colada left on the tabletop. "It sounds like they were close to El Demonio, though. Wouldn't life rafts have helped in that case?"

"Actually, that's not a bad point," Quinn conceded. "No one survived the voyage, though. We have no idea exactly what happened, but apparently it wasn't good."

"You're excited about this to the extreme." Rowan's eyes sparkled. "I'm kind of excited, too. It's something I'll be able to share with you."

"That's the plan." Quinn snagged Rowan's hand and linked his fingers with hers. "I hope they don't take too long to cook the food. I really am excited to get back to the ship. I'm totally going to get you naked before we even look at the book."

Rowan chuckled as a figure moved up to the side of the table and fixed Quinn with a humorous look.

"Oh, you're a smooth talker, aren't you?"

Sally Jenkins, the head of the culinary department on The

Bounding Storm, planted her hands on her hips as she stared down Rowan and Quinn.

Quinn was genuinely fond of Sally, but he internally groaned when she made her presence known. "What are you doing here?"

"Having dinner."

"This is a romantic restaurant," Quinn pointed out. "Are you saying you're in love with yourself and eating alone?"

Sally merely shrugged, unbothered by Quinn's tone. "Would you have a problem with that?"

"No."

"Well, I'm not eating alone." Sally smirked at Quinn's obvious discomfort. "I have a dinner date, although it's not of the romantic variety."

"Who?" Quinn craned his neck, his frown becoming more pronounced when he recognized the man walking in their direction. "Demarcus? He's your date?"

Sally shrugged. "Sometimes the best dinner companions are also the best friends you have in your arsenal. Since I knew Rowan was busy tonight, that left Demarcus as my date."

"Oh, you say the sweetest things, Sally." Demarcus Johnson, The Bounding Storm's head bartender and one of the closest people Quinn had to a confidant on the ship, sauntered to Sally's side and scanned the table. "It looks like you guys have room for two more."

Quinn immediately balked. "We're having a private dinner."

"You two have more private time than an army recruit," Demarcus drawled, grinning at his lame joke. "You'll live." He rounded to the back of the table and took the spot between Quinn and Rowan, allowing Sally to take the spot across the way. "So, what did you two do today?"

Sally and Demarcus plastered bright smiles on their faces, refusing to let Quinn's attitudinal shift affect them.

"We went shopping," Rowan replied. She was torn between mirth and disappointment. She'd had a wonderful day with Quinn.

Tomorrow they would set sail for a whole new type of adventure. She was looking forward to a quiet evening alone, just the two of them. On the other hand, of course, Sally and Demarcus were always entertaining. One meal couldn't possibly hurt them. "I bought a new dress."

"Oh, I can't wait to see it." Sally was enthusiastic. "What else did you do?"

"Quinn gave me a history lesson on the shipwreck we're going to be seeing," Rowan replied. "I found it fascinating."

"Yeah, you guys need to drink more so the things you find fascinating are a little wilder than history lessons," Demarcus drawled. "Speaking of that, though, look who's over there." He inclined his chin to the far corner of the patio, causing everyone to turn and stare in that direction.

"It's Michael," Quinn said after a beat, referring to The Bounding Storm's captain. "You've seen him before."

"I have, and he's a total dreamboat," Demarcus drawled, making a face. "I was talking about the person with Michael."

Rowan stared at the man in question, something about his thinning hair and strong profile causing a jolt of recognition. "Who is that?"

Demarcus turned to her. "He's the head of the group that will be exploring the wreckage of The Conqueror. I think it's called Outer Boundaries or something. I forget his name, though."

"Nicholas Green," Sally supplied. "He came into the kitchen today to go over the menu options. For the first time in I don't know how long, I found someone who wants fewer options when it comes to food choices."

Quinn knit his eyebrows. "Why would he want that?"

"He says that he doesn't want to turn mealtime into a thing," Sally explained. "The main reason they secured The Bounding Storm rather than simply finding private transportation and staying in a hotel is that the accommodations on El Demonio aren't even two stars so they needed a place for the crew to stay that wasn't a bug-infested rat hole. They decided renting an entire ship was the way to go."

"I guess that makes sense in a weird way," Quinn mused. "My understanding is that the wreck isn't far offshore. We'll dock at the island and then they'll take smaller ships to the wreckage."

Rowan was understandably disappointed. "Does that mean we won't be able to see the wreckage?"

"I'll figure a way to get us both out there. Don't worry about that."

"Yes, because there's no way Quinn is going to miss seeing that ship," Demarcus teased. "I haven't seen him this excited for anything since he finally got up the courage to strip you naked, Rowan."

Rowan's cheeks were back to burning. "Um … ."

"Don't say things like that to her," Quinn chided. "She's easily embarrassed."

"You were telling her you wanted to get her naked when I walked up to the table," Sally pointed out.

"Privately," Quinn clarified. "I was telling her that privately. We were trying to have a romantic dinner."

"You can still have a romantic dinner." Demarcus was blasé. "Now you're simply having it with two additional people instead of just Rowan."

"Oh, well, that makes everything totally better." Sarcasm practically dripped off Quinn's tongue as he turned his full attention to Rowan. To his surprise, she remained focused on Michael's table rather than the entertaining conversation flowing freely around her. "What are you looking at, Ro?"

"What?" Rowan shook herself out of her reverie as she turned back to Quinn. She'd been lost in thought and missed the bulk of the most recent chatter. "What did you say?"

"What are you looking at?" Quinn turned his full attention back to Nicholas and Michael. "Do you know him?"

Rowan was sheepish. "I don't think so. I was trying to figure that out myself. There's something familiar about him, though. I can't put my finger on it."

"Maybe you read about him in the newspaper," Quinn suggested. "This find has been all over the front page. I had a copy of the Herald out yesterday and I'm almost positive that guy was in the photo that accompanied the article."

"That's probably it." Rowan forced a smile that didn't quite make it to her eyes. "I'm sure it's not important."

"He was also on the news last night," Sally offered helpfully. "I only know because I was watching it and was surprised when his face popped up."

"You also could've seen him on board earlier today and not even realized it," Demarcus added. "Sometimes you push things like that out of your head until you're reminded of it later."

"I'm sure that's it." Rowan felt a bit goofy for causing a fuss. "It's not a big deal. It's not as if I know him. He simply looked familiar and I couldn't place him. It was like a weird case of déjà vu."

"Well, don't worry about it," Quinn said. "I'm sure you'll figure it out. As for you two ... ." He pointedly shifted his gaze to Sally and Demarcus. "You're ruining our dinner. Move to a different table."

Instead of doing as he asked, Sally merely rolled her eyes. "No. I want to have dinner with Rowan."

"I want to have dinner with her, too," Quinn argued.

"You are having dinner with her. You're just having it with us at the same time."

Quinn made a disgusted sound in the back of his throat. "Why can't you just leave us be?"

"Because you guys spend far too much time wrapped up in each other while shutting out the rest of the world," Demarcus answered. "It was adorable for the first two weeks. It was mildly cute for the second two weeks. Now it's just getting old."

"You're getting old," Quinn shot back.

"You make me feel old," Demarcus corrected. "Stop being an old man. Enjoy the night."

"We were enjoying our night."

Demarcus ignored Quinn's tone. "I'll teach you how to do it better."

"Ugh. You make me tired."

"Right back at you."

Even as Demarcus and Quinn's verbal sparring continued – and Rowan legitimately enjoyed it a great deal – she found her eyes moving back to the man with Michael. She couldn't shake the idea that she knew him and yet she was almost positive they'd never been introduced. It was an odd feeling.

"Right, Rowan?"

At the sound of her name, Rowan swiftly turned back and found Quinn staring. She had no idea what they were talking about, but she agreed all the same. "Absolutely."

Quinn smirked at her answer, but he couldn't stop himself from worrying when Rowan's eyes drifted back to Nicholas Green. What was going on here?

3
THREE

The buzz on the ship was different the next morning and Rowan couldn't contain her excitement as she and Quinn readied to separate for the next few hours.

"There's a different feel in the atmosphere," she observed. "I'm not sure how to describe it."

Quinn, who had been up early to look at his book since he didn't have a chance the night before, merely nodded. "It won't be like the other trips you've been on."

Rowan was curious. "Have you been on a trip like this one before?"

"No, but I think I know better what to expect. You're still getting used to the everyday operations of The Bounding Storm. Everything is new to you."

"That thing you did last night was definitely new," Rowan teased.

Quinn was confused. "Which thing?"

"The part where you waited until you thought I was asleep to look at your book."

Quinn pressed his lips together to keep from laughing. "I thought you were out."

Rowan patted his arm in a soothing manner. "Don't worry about it. I found it cute."

"In my defense, it was a very interesting book."

"I'm sure it was." Rowan was beyond delighted by his reaction. "Speaking of everyday operations, though, am I supposed to take photographs of these people? I know they're here for a job but ... I'm not sure what I'm supposed to be doing. No one has broken it down for me."

Quinn rubbed the back of his neck as he considered the question. "I would take photos," he said after a beat. "If this discovery is as big as I think it's going to be, they'll probably want something to remember the trip by. I don't think you need to take photos during meals or anything, but head to the lobby for check-in and hit the deck once we set sail."

"We're not going to be on the open water for a long time, though. What happens when we dock? Will the boat be empty for the bulk of the day while everyone is off exploring The Conqueror?"

Quinn shrugged. "I don't know. I'll ask around today and see if I can get an answer for you. I'm going to guess that a lot of people will remain on the ship because they'll have their own tasks to do, but I'm honestly not sure. I'll find out, though."

"Okay." Rowan flashed a pretty smile. "I suppose I should head to the lobby then. People are due to start arriving in about twenty minutes."

"Yeah, I need to check in with Michael and then I want to talk to the people heading up the dives. I think it's best if we touch base even though they're technically outside of my operational realm."

"You're nothing if not diligent."

Rowan couldn't hide her smile and it made Quinn nervous.

"What aren't you saying?"

"You want to talk to the people heading the dive because you're a geek," Rowan replied without hesitation. "Just admit it."

Quinn balked. "I have a job to do."

would be able to close off that entire area so only those with access will be granted entrance. Since there won't be random guests on the ship, it shouldn't be a problem, right?"

"It shouldn't be." Quinn was all business. "The salon is located down its own private hallway. There's nothing down there except for a rest room. We can close off both ends of the hallway and position guards there.

"Then we can issue key cards to specific members of your team," he continued. "You can supply us with names and we can make up the proper cards right on the ship. Between the cards and keycard scanners, we should be able to close off the entire area."

"That's exactly what I'm looking for." Nick beamed. "This is going to turn into a big deal. I can feel it in my bones. The last time a ship of this age was discovered in an area so close to land was ... well, a long time ago."

"Yes, Quinn here has been boning up on the history of The Conqueror," Michael offered. "He's a bit of a history fanatic."

Quinn cleared his throat, uncomfortable. "I wouldn't call myself a fanatic."

"What would you call yourself?"

"Intrigued," Quinn replied easily. "I'm looking forward to seeing the site. You said you were bringing your own security on board – which makes sense – but I would like to touch base with the head once he's settled. I want to make sure we're on the same page."

"That should be easy to arrange," Nick said. "He should be here in about an hour."

"Until then, Nick wants a tour of the ship," Michael supplied. "I have a few things going on so I can't do it. Do you think you can handle that, Quinn?"

Quinn didn't fancy himself a tour guide, but he was anxious to get to know Nick better – if only because the man had the inside track on the ship discovery – so he eagerly nodded his head. "I can definitely handle that."

"Great." Nick pushed himself to a standing position. "Let's get started."

ROWAN RARELY FOUND HERSELF bored on The Bounding Storm but that's exactly how she felt as she leaned against the lobby counter and watched people check in. Not one of them had wanted their photograph taken – and more than a few had laughed at the notion. Instead of asking, Rowan had taken to shooting candid photographs of people as they entered and left. She wanted to justify her salary and that's the only way she could think to do it.

"This one is going to be really different, huh?" Vicky Salisbury, one of the regular mainstays at the front desk, looked as bored as Rowan felt as she asked the question.

Rowan nodded. "I don't think there's going to be a lot of jewelry shopping or fun party nights happening. Er, well, I guess there might be some fun party nights when the searches are done for the day. I think it's likely they'll be happening on deck rather than in the dining room, though."

"Yeah. I wasn't sure what to expect, but it wasn't this. These people aren't on vacation so they haven't been doing a lot of smiling. They seem intense to me."

Rowan couldn't argue with the sentiment. "Well, it's supposed to be a big find. I don't know a lot about salvage operations like this, but Quinn does and he's really excited."

Vicky brightened at the conversational shift. "How is Quinn? And by that, I mean how is he in bed?"

The question caught Rowan off guard. "Excuse me?"

"Oh, don't play coy." Vicky was in no mood for games. "He's hot, handsome, and he looks like he has stamina. Everyone was chasing him from here to the Bahamas every chance they got before you showed up. Okay, some might still be chasing him, but most have stepped back and realized that he only has eyes for you.

"That doesn't mean we're not curious," she continued. "He's ridiculously hot and inquiring minds want to know so ... share."

Rowan was both amused and flabbergasted. "I don't kiss and tell."

"Yeah? I don't care about the kissing. Tell me about the other stuff."

Rowan shook her head. "Okay, I'm done here. I'm going to head to the deck and take some candid photos. No one wants the staged ones and I need something to do."

"I've already given you another option for something to do."

"I want something to do that doesn't make me feel skeevy," Rowan shot back as she moved toward the door. "I hope the rest of your afternoon is more entertaining."

"There's not much chance of that since you refuse to gossip."

Rowan chuckled to herself, genuinely amused that her relationship with Quinn was the focal point of ship gossip for so many people, as she headed for the deck. She was lost in thought, ideas for what she could do with Quinn and his new book once dinner was over with flitting through her head, when she accidentally crashed into the man in question as she moved to head toward the tiki bar.

Quinn instinctively reached out and grabbed her before she could overcompensate in the opposite direction and fall to the ground.

"Holy crap," Rowan sputtered as she tried to regain her footing. "That was ... divine intervention or something."

Quinn cocked an eyebrow as he steadied her. "You should watch where you're going. It's not that I don't like to save a damsel in distress, but I wouldn't be happy if you hurt yourself if I wasn't around to catch you."

Rowan made a hilarious face. "Ha, ha. I was distracted. I'm sorry."

Quinn grinned as he removed his hands. "You're always distracted."

"I am and I can't help it. In fact ... ." Rowan was about to go off on a diatribe about Vicky's questions when she realized Quinn wasn't alone. Nicholas Green was with him, a wide and friendly smile on the man's face, and she was struck with a wave of familiarity for the second time while looking at him. "Oh, you're working."

"I am," Quinn confirmed, his eyes curious as they bounced between Nick and Rowan. He could tell she was still trying to place where she knew the man from – none of the options from the previous evening seemed to appeal to her – and Quinn was understandably curious himself. "I'm giving Mr. Green a tour and then I'm going to meet the security chief he's bringing along for the ship site."

"Oh." Rowan had no idea what that meant. "Well, it's nice to meet you." She extended her hand and smiled when Nick grasped it. "I hope you get everything you want out of this trip. I hear it's going to be quite the extravaganza."

"Yes, it should be." Nick kept his eyes trained on Rowan's face – something that Quinn didn't miss but opted not to comment on – and widened his grin until it was so big Quinn thought it might fall off his face. "And you are?"

"Oh, excuse my manners." Quinn was embarrassed. "This is Rowan Gray. She's the ship photographer."

"Oh, well, that's exciting." Nick kept his smile in place. "You probably won't have a lot to do on the ship this go around, but if you're interested in taking photographs of the dive site as the workers bring up items, I think everyone would benefit from that."

Rowan was excited by the offer, but she looked to Quinn before answering.

"I don't see why that would be a problem," Quinn said after a beat. "You want photos and there's going to be nothing for Rowan to shoot on board once we get to El Demonio. I want to look at the setup and make sure she'll be safe, but I'm sure I can arrange for her to be there. Heck, maybe I'll even go to act as her personal security representative."

Rowan bit the inside of her cheek to keep from laughing. While she had no doubt that Quinn wanted to keep her safe, she was equally convinced that he wanted to see the site just as much. If he could accomplish both, his world would essentially be perfect.

"I'll talk about it with Anthony when he gets here, but given your military background, Quinn, I doubt he'll have a problem with your presence," Nick offered.

"Who is Anthony?" Rowan asked, knitting her brow.

"Anthony Lowell," Nick supplied. "He's going to be heading up security on the water site while Quinn handles operations in the salon."

"The salon?" Rowan was confused. "What's happening in the salon?"

Quinn was too focused on Nick to answer the question. "Did you just say Anthony Lowell is handling the security?"

Nick nodded. "Why? Do you know him?"

"I know *of* him," Quinn clarified. "He's got quite the reputation in certain circles."

Quinn's reaction was so hard to read Rowan couldn't contain her bafflement. "A good reputation or a bad reputation?"

The question wasn't easy for Quinn to answer. "A strong reputation," he said finally. "He's kind of the top of the heap in personal security."

"He is," Nick agreed. "He also has a reputation as a bit of a hardass."

"He does." Quinn bobbed his head. "I'm impressed that he's the one who is handling security on this, though. From what I understand, Lowell is extremely expensive to put on retainer."

"Yes, but this is a very important find," Nick explained. "Lowell already has a freelance team out watching the site. You have to understand, when something of this magnitude is discovered, every pirate between here and Europe will descend on this particular area in the hope of finding treasure."

"The money you were telling me about last night?" Rowan asked Quinn.

"Yes," Quinn confirmed. "It makes for an enticing target even though the site has been declared off limits. Professional divers, the ones who know what they're doing, will try to come in from all sides under the water to loot the site. It's a pain to keep people clear."

"So that's why you need security," Rowan mused. "It sounds like an exciting adventure, even if it is potentially dangerous."

"Once everyone is in place, I think the danger will be minimalized," Nick said. "That's why I want you and Anthony to get to know one another, though, Quinn. You'll both be in charge of different legs of our security."

"I'm anxious to meet him." Quinn flashed a smile before turning to Rowan. "What are you doing for the rest of the afternoon?"

"Well, no one wants staged cruise photos, so I figured I would go to the deck and take candid shots. I feel the need to earn my salary even if I'm not technically earning my salary."

Quinn chuckled. "Don't worry about it. No one is going to say anything. I promise you that."

"I still want to take some photos."

"Okay, well, I should be clear in time for dinner. I'll find you before then and we'll head to the dining room together."

Rowan mock saluted. "I'm looking forward to it."

"Yeah, yeah." Quinn rolled his eyes as he watched her go, eventually flicking his gaze to Nick and finding that the man was equally entranced with Rowan. "You almost look as if you recognize her."

Nick jolted at the words, his sloppy grin back as he shook his head. "I wish. She's a beautiful woman. She seems to have a nice personality, too."

"She does." Quinn wanted to believe Nick was merely entranced by Rowan's beauty, but he sensed something else going on. He simply couldn't put a name to it. "Should we continue our tour?"

"Definitely. Let's get at it."

4

FOUR

"So, that's your girlfriend, huh?"

Nick asked the question in an easy manner, but Quinn's antenna was up and he sensed the man's interest stemmed from something other than polite curiosity. For the life of him, though, he couldn't imagine what.

"She is," Quinn confirmed.

"She's very pretty."

"I think so." Quinn licked his lips. "You seemed to like what you saw at least."

Nick balked. "I was merely looking at her because you saved her from falling. I didn't mean any offense."

"I didn't take offense. I was just surprised how hard you stared. For a second, I thought you guys might know each other from someplace else."

"That would be quite the coincidence, wouldn't it? Alas, I believe this was the first time I ever laid eyes on her."

"We were at the same restaurant you were last night," Quinn offered. "We saw you with Michael."

"Oh, well, that's nice. I wish I would've had the chance to meet you then."

Nick remained friendly but there was something standoffish about his attitude. The notion set Quinn's teeth on edge.

"Yeah, well, we were with friends." Quinn rolled his neck until it cracked. "Where do you want to look next?"

"I've heard mention of a tiki bar."

"Sure. That sounds good."

ROWAN SNAPPED PHOTOS for an hour before taking refuge from the sun in the shade offered by the covered tiki bar. Demarcus was behind the bar and he shoved a fresh glass of iced tea in front of her before she requested it.

"How did you know I wanted this?"

"Because you're hot and sweaty and that's what you always order," Demarcus replied without hesitation. "How has your afternoon been?"

"Not great. No one wants their photo taken because they consider this work and not play."

"So treat it like a vacation week," Demarcus suggested. "That's what I would do."

"I feel guilty even considering that."

"Because you're a good girl?"

"Because ... um ... I was hired for a job."

Demarcus rolled his eyes. "You really are a good girl. I guess it makes sense. Quinn is a good guy. Together you're so vanilla that it's almost blinding."

Rowan had no idea if Demarcus meant for the statement to be insulting but that's exactly how she took it. "We're not vanilla. We're ... yummy, yummy chocolate. With marshmallows and hot fudge. And peanuts. And those cool cherries you put on top."

Demarcus realized his mistake too late to take it back. "Okay, I shouldn't have said that." He dug in the garnish tray to his right and came back with four maraschino cherries on a napkin. "I apologize. You're not vanilla. You're totally ... chocolate chip cookie dough ice cream."

Rowan rolled her eyes as she popped one of the cherries into her mouth. "I know you don't mean that, but we totally are."

Demarcus chuckled. "Definitely." He shifted his eyes to the deck, something catching his attention. "Who is that guy with Quinn? I can't quite make him out."

Rowan followed his gaze, frowning when she caught sight of Nick. "Nicholas Green."

"You don't look happy about them hanging out."

"I'm not unhappy. I just ... have you ever had a case of déjà vu?"

The shift in conversation caught Demarcus off guard. "I guess."

"I have this feeling that I met him somewhere – like long ago in my past – but I can't put my finger on where."

"You used to work for a newspaper, right?"

Rowan nodded.

"Maybe you took his photograph for a story and you don't remember simply because it was a long time ago," Demarcus suggested. "I mean ... how many stories did you cover during your tenure at that newspaper?"

"Hundreds," Rowan conceded. "I guess it's possible but ... he investigates shipwrecks. I lived in Michigan. We don't have a lot of shipwrecks."

Demarcus snorted, the sound both derisive and full of mirth at the same time. "Honey, Michigan is surrounded by lakes. Do you have any idea how many shipwrecks there are in the Great Lakes?"

"I ... ." Rowan wanted to argue but she couldn't. Instead she trailed off in frustration. "You're totally right. There are hundreds of shipwrecks in the lakes and whenever a new one was discovered, they made a big deal about it. That includes pictures and news stories."

"That's probably where you know him from. He seems like an amiable enough guy, by the way. Just ask him if he was ever interviewed by your newspaper."

"That seems like a randomly weird thing to ask him about."

"Yes, but you're a randomly weird chick." Demarcus grinned when Rowan's smile slipped. "Geez. You're having absolutely zero fun today. What gives?"

"I'm having fun," Rowan argued. "I woke up in a great mood. Quinn got a book about shipwrecks and he's so excited about it. It talks about the history of the ships that crossed over during the Revolutionary War and The Conqueror was one of them. He's so keyed up I'm surprised he doesn't do a little dance."

"You guys really found each other, didn't you?" Demarcus asked dryly. "Only you two would get excited about a book."

"Oh, whatever." Rowan sipped her iced tea. "I'm glad he's so excited. If he likes shipwrecks, more power to him."

"You think he's kind of a geek, too, don't you?"

Rowan pursed her lips. "I happen to like geeks."

Demarcus snorted. "Of course you do." He turned his attention to a ridiculously tall man wearing a tight black T-shirt. The man was so big his biceps looked like torpedoes and his chiseled jaw appeared as if it might have been carved out of granite. "Can I get you something?"

"I'll have a Jack and Coke," the man replied, his voice low and gravelly. "I need to open a tab, too." He offered up his room card. "I can just charge it to my room, right?"

Demarcus nodded. "Absolutely. Let me run that real quick." Demarcus slid the card through the register before returning it to the counter. "I'll have your drink in just a minute."

Since Demarcus was busy and the man was so big Rowan felt uncomfortable sitting in silence, his frame hulking over hers, she offered up a lame greeting.

"You're absolutely huge."

Demarcus did his best to bite back a laugh ... and failed miserably. Luckily for Rowan, the man in question appeared amused by her observation.

"Strangely enough, you're not the first one to tell me that."

Rowan flicked her eyes to the card and widened them when she read the name. "Anthony Lowell, huh? You're heading the security of the wreck site."

Anthony couldn't help being impressed. "I am. How did you know that?"

"I'm the ship photographer. I hear things."

"She's also sleeping with the head of security," Demarcus offered as he slid a drink in front of Anthony. "She's got big ears and her boyfriend is so geeked over this ship find that it's almost pathetic."

If Anthony thought Demarcus was over-sharing – which Rowan happened to believe – he didn't show it. "So you're the ship's photographer and attached to the head of security. It sounds like you live a busy life."

"Oh, don't patronize me," Rowan chided, wagging a finger. "You guys are going to be boring guests because you don't want any photos. I'm drinking iced tea in the middle of the afternoon. We both know I'm not busy."

Anthony chuckled, the sound low and inviting. "Well, at least you're honest."

"Your boss wants to utilize me to take photos of the site once we get there. Nicholas Green. He talked to me a little bit ago. That's at least something."

"You've seen Nick?" Anthony cocked an interested eyebrow. "You don't happen to know where he is, do you?"

Rowan extended a finger and pointed toward the deck. Anthony followed it, his expression unreadable.

"Do you know who he's with?"

"That would be Rowan's love dolphin," Demarcus supplied, making a face when Rowan pinned him with a dark look. "What? You look like the dolphin type. Sue me."

Rowan sucked in a steadying breath before speaking. She was afraid she would verbally lambast Demarcus if she didn't. "That's Quinn Davenport. He's head of security."

"Davenport, huh? I think I recognize that name."

The admission surprised Rowan. "You do?"

"He was big in security overseas, right? Afghanistan?"

Rowan was embarrassed to admit she had no idea. "I don't ... know." She turned to Demarcus for help and the generally verbose bartender could do nothing but shrug. "He doesn't talk about his military time very often."

When Anthony turned back to Rowan, his expression was thoughtful. "I can see that. If it's the guy I'm thinking about, we never crossed paths but we did a lot of the same things while we were over there."

Rowan's gaze drifted to Anthony's huge muscles. "I don't think Quinn did all the same things you did."

Demarcus chuckled. "Oh, I can't wait to tell Quinn that his woman is checking out another guy. He's going to have an absolute meltdown."

Rowan straightened her back, annoyed. "I am not checking him out. I'm perfectly happy with Quinn. In fact, I happen to think his muscles are better than this guy's muscles – no offense – because this guy's muscles are freaky. He looks like a reject from an old Arnold Schwarzenegger movie. You know that one where they're hunting aliens in the rain forest? He looks like he could be one of the hunters ... or the alien. He's got torpedoes for arms."

"That's what I thought, too," Demarcus said, grinning.

Rowan was almost breathless by the time she finished her diatribe. Instead of being offended – or even irritated – Anthony laughed so hard he drew a multitude of gazes from various tables as he slapped the bar.

"I like you," Anthony announced, his face lit with mirth. "If you didn't already have a boyfriend, one you seem to be rather fond of, I would be all over you."

"I guess it's good she has a boyfriend then," Quinn announced, appearing behind Rowan.

His arrival was enough to cause Rowan's cheeks to burn and

when she turned in his direction, her face was on fire. "I was just explaining that I'm not turned on by him."

Quinn had no idea what to make of the statement. "I'm sorry but ... what?"

"Oh, this is going to be priceless." Demarcus rested his hands on the bar, his shoulders shaking with silent laughter.

"I was just explaining I wasn't attracted to him," Rowan repeated. "For the record, I'm not."

"I see." Quinn didn't see, but he wasn't sure he wanted to press the issue.

"Oh, don't get your boxers in a bunch," Demarcus admonished. "I'm the one who started it. Rowan couldn't stop looking at his arms and her way of introducing herself was to comment on the fact that he was huge."

Quinn cracked a smile. "Oh."

"She's kind of a spaz. Since you're kind of a spaz, you guys are perfect for each other."

"I'm not a spaz," Quinn corrected.

"You're supposed to say I'm not a spaz either," Rowan supplied.

"You're definitely a spaz," Quinn said. "I'm fine with it, though." He turned his full attention to Anthony, instinctively squaring his shoulders as he did. The man *was* huge. There was no getting around that. Quinn often fancied himself the strongest man in the room, but he was fairly certain Rowan's new friend could crush him without breaking a sweat. "I'm Quinn Davenport." He extended his hand.

Anthony gladly shook it, amusement coursing through him. "Anthony Lowell. I absolutely love your girlfriend, by the way."

"Yes, well, she's a unique soul." Quinn debated which seat to take and ultimately picked the spot on the other side of Anthony. He didn't want the man to think he was marking his territory by crowding Rowan. "I heard you were going to be running security at the site. I've been wanting to meet you for some time."

"So you are the Quinn Davenport who ran that operation in

Afghanistan." Anthony looked impressed as Rowan adopted a curious expression.

Demarcus was the one to ask the obvious question. "What's the operation in Afghanistan?"

"It's classified," Quinn and Anthony answered in unison.

"Oh, well, sorry." Demarcus made an exaggerated face as he shoved an iced tea in front of Quinn. "I assume you're still on duty."

Quinn bobbed his head in thanks. "You assume right." He sipped the iced tea. "I just spent an hour with your boss. He seems on top of things."

"I've only worked with him twice," Anthony explained. "He's new to the salvage company and I'm freelance, so I'm only hired for specific gigs. From what I can tell, he's easy to work with and willing to step up when the job calls for a firm hand."

"Do you expect this job to require a firm hand?" Rowan asked.

Anthony shrugged. "I might have to dust off my torpedoes and fire them." He winked at her, amused by her obvious discomfort. "Honestly, though, I am worried that pirates might approach on the water. I have no knowledge that will happen, but it's in the back of my head."

"I'm going to make sure no one who isn't authorized can get into the salon, post guards at both doors, but I'm not sure we can stop interested parties from boarding the ship altogether," Quinn said. "Usually when we go to port, people come on and off as they wish. We check rooms before leaving but … I'm starting to think we're going to need someone watching the entry point to The Bounding Storm, too."

"That's not a bad idea," Anthony agreed. "We have no idea how much money was on The Conqueror. We also have no idea how much money we're going to find. So far we've found a few coins and they're worth more than a hundred grand, but we're dealing with a unique set of circumstances here."

"What's unique about it?" Rowan asked, doing her best not to be agitated because Quinn chose to sit next to Anthony rather than her.

She considered herself too mature to have her nose out of joint regarding something so trivial, but it irked all the same.

"Well, for starters, the ship being close to land like it is probably means that the water was extremely rough at times," Anthony answered. "The tides are known to be brutal in that area, which is why we need a very specialized dive team. Because of the rough waves, when the boat disintegrated – and from what I've heard, very little is left that hasn't turned into coral – that means the coins were eventually scattered because the boxes and chests they were kept in disintegrated, too."

"Oh." Rowan found the conversation fascinating. "If the coins are spread about, do you think you'll find them?"

Anthony held his hands palms up and shrugged. "We're hopeful we'll be able to find a lot of things – not just the coins – but it's too soon to tell."

"Will you dive?" Quinn asked.

"I will at some point, but the first day is going to be all about setting up the proper security. That's the most important thing. We don't want people running off with the relics."

"If the water is so treacherous there, aren't you worried about people dying in the dive attempt?" Rowan asked.

"Yes, and no," Anthony replied. "My understanding is that Nick brought in Andrea Morgan to lead the dive team."

"He did," Quinn confirmed. "He's over talking to her now."

Anthony glanced over his shoulder and took in the willowy brunette. She was beautiful even from a distance and Rowan couldn't stop herself from sucking in her gut when she caught sight of her thin frame.

"I'm going to want to sit down and make a plan with her," Anthony said. "She's supposed to know her stuff. We've never worked together before."

"How come she was called in on this if she's a new face?" Rowan asked.

"Because Nick wanted the best and apparently that's her. This could be the biggest deal in decades, maybe even centuries, if we find everything Nick is hoping we find."

"You don't look as if you think it's going to be an easy job," Rowan noted.

"I don't think it's going to be easy at all. In fact, I think it's going to be downright difficult. We'll do our best, though. This is a fluid situation and we're all going to have to be ready to shift on a dime if it becomes necessary."

"Let's just hope it doesn't become necessary," Quinn said.

Anthony nodded. "I'm right there with you."

FIVE

"Do you want to tell me about your new friend?"

Quinn watched Rowan survey her image in the full-length mirror in her quarters, his arms crossed over his chest and an unreadable look on his face. They'd separated for the bulk of the afternoon – Quinn had a job to do, after all, and he wouldn't allow that to fall by the wayside – but he remained bothered by what happened with Rowan and Anthony at the tiki bar.

Rowan wrinkled her forehead. "What new friend? Are you talking about Vicky? If she said something to you, I told her there was no way I was going to talk about your performance in bed."

Now it was Quinn's turn to be confused. "I'm sorry but ... what?"

"What were you talking about?" Rowan asked, legitimately quizzical.

"What were you talking about?" Quinn shot back.

"I was talking about my time in the lobby this afternoon," Rowan replied without hesitation. "You know that Vicky girl at the front desk? Suddenly she wants to be my best friend and she wouldn't stop asking me about you. It was a ridiculous situation ... and she is so not my friend."

Quinn opened his mouth, unsure what to say. "Oh, well ... huh."

"Huh, what?"

"I was about to have a little fit about the way you flirted with Anthony this afternoon, but you don't even remember it so now I'm starting to wonder if I'm being absurd."

The simple statement caught Rowan off guard. "I wasn't flirting with him."

"He made it seem like you were."

"Well, I wasn't. I was sticking my foot in my mouth – that's nothing new – but I definitely wasn't flirting with him."

"You commented on his arms."

"Because he looks as if he has the worst case of mumps ever."

Quinn couldn't stay angry – not that he really was – and simply made a clucking sound with his tongue as he shook his head. "You are something."

"I know." Rowan moved to stand in front of Quinn, her expression hard to read. "You don't trust me, huh?"

Quinn immediately balked. "Of course I trust you. I didn't think you were going to move on Anthony. It's just ... he seemed enamored with you."

"I think it's more that he thought I was funny because I blurted out the thing about his arms. Given his size, he's probably used to people walking on eggshells around him. Instead of doing that, I said something completely stupid and for some reason that put him at ease."

"Perhaps it has a little something to do with your smile."

"Or perhaps he thinks I'm goofy." Rowan tilted her head to the side, considering. "If you don't trust me ... ."

Quinn shook his head to cut her off. "I trust you. I'm sorry if I made you think otherwise. I was caught off guard seeing you with him. You're right about him being huge, by the way. All I could think was that if he made a move on you I would probably die trying to defend your honor."

Rowan snorted, amused by his hangdog expression. "Did you

consider that you don't need to defend my honor because I'm capable of taking care of myself?"

"No." Quinn answered immediately. "You're my girlfriend. The second I saw you I got jealous. I have no idea why. It was ridiculous and stupid because that guy could kill me with one hand tied behind his back. No, literally he could do it that way."

Rowan snickered, resting her hand on Quinn's solid chest. "I think this entire thing is so big in your head it's hard to adapt to. First you get word that we're going to be hanging around a shipwreck, and you're a total geek for shipwrecks."

"What did I tell you about using the word 'geek'?"

Rowan ignored the question. "Then you find out you'll be sharing security duty. On one hand, you don't like it because you prefer being in charge. On the other, you've been invited to involve yourself in some of the finds from their dives so you're understandably circling uber-geek mode."

"Keep pushing it," Quinn warned.

"Then you meet a guy who has something of a reputation in the circles you used to run in." Rowan turned thoughtful. "He was famous and yet he knows about you. He knows something you did that impresses him – something you can't talk about, mind you – and you're kind of embarrassed and pleased at the same time."

"I can't talk about that," Quinn cautioned. "It's classified."

"I know. It only hurts a little."

Quinn frowned at the way Rowan's lips curved. "Don't go there." He didn't want to encourage her, but the pout was beyond sexy and he couldn't stop himself from planting a firm kiss on her lips. "I can't talk about it."

"I know."

"Even if I could ... ." Quinn took on a far-off expression before shaking himself out of his reverie. "It's not a big deal."

"Neither was what I said to Anthony," Rowan offered. "It was stupid more than anything else. I'm just glad I didn't pull out my inappropriate Hulk humor."

Quinn cocked an amused eyebrow. "You have inappropriate Hulk humor?"

"I have a ton of it."

He grinned and held out his hand. "How about you tell me some of it on our way to dinner?"

Sensing the crisis had passed – if there was ever really a crisis rather than random irritation – Rowan slipped her hand in his and walked with him to the door. "Did I ever mention I love the color green and you wouldn't like me when I'm angry?"

Quinn snorted. "Oh, well, I can't wait to hear this."

QUINN EXPECTED TO **HAVE** a quiet meal with Rowan. Instead, he found Anthony sitting at a corner table with Andrea Morgan – who was even more striking up close – and the security guru waved Quinn over so he had no choice but to greet them.

"You should sit with us," Anthony announced. "We're talking about the dive site and the salon so we want to bounce some ideas off you."

"Oh, well ... ." Quinn cast a glance over his shoulder to the buffet line where Rowan was filling her plate with fresh seafood.

Anthony followed his gaze and smiled. "Are you on a date?"

"It's not so much a date as dinner, but we usually eat alone," Quinn replied. "I'm sure Rowan won't mind all of us eating together, though."

"Does she have clearance?" Andrea wrinkled her nose. "What does she even do on this ship?"

Quinn didn't like the woman's attitude. "She's the ship photographer. If you don't want her here, we can eat elsewhere."

"Or you can send her elsewhere," Andrea argued.

"Yeah, that's not going to happen." Quinn was adamant. "We can meet tomorrow morning and go over the plans. We have plenty of time to get everything in position. We're not under the gun."

"Wait a second." Anthony shot Andrea a dark look. "We can talk tonight. No one meant any offense about Rowan."

Quinn didn't believe that for a second. "Yeah, well, we'll have a meeting after breakfast tomorrow."

"I honestly think we should do a little talking now," Anthony pressed. "I don't want to ruin your night but ... it's a big deal."

"I'm well aware of that." Quinn ran his tongue over his teeth as he watched Rowan laugh with a man in the buffet line. The simple act lit up her entire face. "I'm eating dinner with her. You can either wait until after dinner to talk or do it in front of her."

"We can talk in front of her." Anthony appeared to be easygoing, but Quinn was aware of his reputation so he knew it was an act.

"Are we sure we can trust her?" Andrea asked.

Quinn scowled as Anthony held up a hand to quiet him.

"I've met her," Anthony said. "She seems ... ridiculously fun. There's no reason to get worked up about it. What do you think she's going to do?"

Andrea held her hands palms out and shrugged. "You're in charge of security."

"I am," Anthony agreed. "Go ahead and get Rowan."

Quinn wasn't happy about the change in eating circumstances, but he didn't see a way out of the situation. He found Rowan with a pair of tongs, heaping crab legs on her plate, and informed her of what Anthony and Andrea wanted. Surprisingly, she was fine with the change and waited for Quinn to fill a plate before walking over with him.

Even though he didn't want Rowan sitting next to Anthony – he still harbored faint twinges of unexplained jealousy – Quinn worried Andrea might pick a fight with her so he willingly took the open spot next to the famous diver while Rowan settled between him and Anthony.

"I'm going to guess you like crab legs." Anthony's eyes sparkled as he looked at Rowan's dinner spread. "And shrimp and scallops."

"I like seafood but not fish," Rowan conceded. "I have no idea why."

"Fish is better for you," Andrea offered. "You'll clog your arteries with all that butter you're using as dipping sauce."

Quinn internally cringed, expecting Rowan to say something snarky. Instead his girlfriend merely shrugged.

"What a way to go, right?"

Andrea opened her mouth, perhaps to say something sarcastic of her own, but instead she snapped her mouth shut and offered up a rueful smile. "I see why Anthony says you're funny." She didn't laugh, but she looked mildly amused. "He said you commented on his torpedoes."

"Well, they're huge." Rowan broke a roll in half and handed a chunk to Quinn. It was a ritual of sorts and she hardly noticed the act seemed to intrigue their dinner companions until Anthony arched an eyebrow. "What?"

"You guys are cute," Anthony said after a beat. "I have to admit, I'm a little sad. After what you said at the tiki bar, I thought for sure I would be able to get you to rub my torpedoes."

Quinn shot him a dirty look. "Don't go there."

Anthony chuckled. "You didn't let me finish. I was going to say that I knew it was a wasted effort after seeing you guys together."

"It's definitely a wasted effort." Quinn rolled his neck until it cracked. He'd been looking forward to a relaxing dinner, but apparently that wasn't on the menu. He had to adjust to that fact and move on. "So, what do you have in mind for the security at the dive site?"

Andrea warmed to her subject quickly, rambling on about a great many things Rowan didn't understand. She wasn't familiar with tides or levels of visibility underwater. She made a show of being interested, but in reality her mind wandered. As it did, she let her gaze drift until it snagged with a set of eyes across the dining room.

She jolted when she realized it was Nick. He sat a good fifty feet away, a group of people chatting around him, but he didn't so much as look in their direction. His attention was completely focused on Rowan ... and it made her uncomfortable.

Rowan used her napkin to wipe the corners of her mouth and then licked her lips as she waited for a break in the conversation. When it finally occurred, she pasted a pleasant smile on her face.

"I'm going to leave you guys to finish up and head out."

"Oh, I'm sorry." Anthony was instantly apologetic. "We're boring you."

"Not in the least," Rowan said hurriedly. "You guys have work to talk about, though, and I want to run up to the tiki bar."

"If you wait a few minutes, I can go with you," Quinn offered. "We're almost done here."

The last thing Rowan wanted was for Quinn to rush through official work on her account. "No. It's perfectly fine. I'll meet you up there when you're done. Sally is supposed to be with Demarcus right about now and I want to talk to her anyway."

Quinn wasn't sure he believed the excuse, but he could hardly blame her for being bored. "Okay, well ... I'll see you in a little bit then." He could feel Andrea and Anthony's eyes on him, which made him feel uncomfortable enough that he didn't offer Rowan a kiss. Thankfully she didn't seem to expect one. "I won't be long."

Rowan's smile was back, but it didn't make it all the way to her eyes. "I will be waiting for you on deck. We'll pick up our date then."

ROWAN HONESTLY DIDN'T EXPECT to find Sally at the tiki bar. The feisty chef generally remained in the kitchen until the meal was over and then headed for the deck when she was sure everyone was happy with their meals. Rowan wasn't anxious to see Sally – or even get away from Andrea and Anthony. No, she was most anxious to get away from Nick's probing stare.

There was definitely something off about the man, although she couldn't determine what.

Demarcus held court behind the bar, entertaining a bevy of

divers as they drank and made merry. Rowan was happy to take a spot in the corner, one that was away from everyone else so she could regroup and gather her wits.

She'd barely sat down when a figure appeared on the other side of the table and stole the breath from her lungs.

"Hello, Ms. Gray."

"Mr. Green," Rowan forced out, her stomach lurching. "I'm surprised to see you up here. I thought I saw you down in the dining room just a few minutes ago."

"Yes, well, I like walking after a meal," Nick said, taking the seat across from Rowan without her uttering an invitation. "It's better for digestion."

"I've heard something like that." Rowan wasn't fearful of Nick. He clearly wasn't about to jump her in front of so many people. She found she couldn't relax around him, though, and her spine stayed ramrod straight. "You must be excited about the dive. All I keep hearing is everyone making plans for security and what they hope to see first."

"Yes, well, finds like this don't happen on a regular basis. The excitement is real and hard to rein in. I'm sure it will diminish a bit once we've been out there for a few days."

"Right."

"What about you?" Nick asked. "Do you dive?"

Rowan immediately started shaking her head. "I have a phobia about suffocating. I don't think I would do well underwater. Plus, well, I'm afraid of sharks."

Nick chuckled. "The odds of being attacked by a shark are much less than being in an automobile accident or drowning."

"Yes, well, that doesn't exactly make me feel better," Rowan noted. "I can't explain it. I'm not sure why I'm so fearful of suffocating. I wasn't phobic about it when I was a kid, but it's something that popped up when I was an adult."

"Perhaps it's from being abandoned," Nick mused, taking Rowan by surprise with his words. "You found yourself alone, the world closing in on you because you couldn't make sense of what was happening. I don't think what you're describing is that out of the ordinary."

Rowan's mouth dropped open. "Excuse me?"

Nick jolted back to reality. "Oh, I'm sorry. I go off at the mouth sometimes. I shouldn't have said that."

Rowan couldn't argue with the sentiment and yet she remained flustered. "How did you know I was abandoned?"

"What? Oh, well, I probably read it in your personnel file and it stuck with me for some reason," Nick said, rising. "I had to read everyone's files when I boarded to acquaint myself with the main staff."

Rowan was dubious. "And my file says I was abandoned as a teenager?"

"Oh, well, it must, right?" Nick turned nervous. "How else would I know that information about you?"

How else indeed? "I don't know." Rowan chose her words carefully. "I can't quite shake the feeling that I know you, or at least I did at one time. Have you ever spent time in Michigan? Perhaps you were interviewed by a Michigan newspaper at one time or something."

"That's certainly a possibility, but I can't remember off the top of my head." Nick shifted his eyes to the deck, two figures catching his attention. "Well, there are some people I must talk to. I'll be taking my leave."

Suddenly Rowan was desperate for him to stay, if only because she wanted answers she believed he could give. "Wait ... ."

"I'm sure I'll see you around." Nick offered up a haphazard wave as he scurried across the deck. "Have a wonderful night. It was a pleasure talking to you."

And just like that he was gone ... and Rowan was left with a mountain of doubt to weigh her down.

SIX

Quinn never showed up at the tiki bar. Rowan had two drinks with Sally and Demarcus and then called it a night. It took every bit of patience she had not to head to the dining room to check on him. He had a job to do, after all. He couldn't simply ignore it.

When she woke alone the next morning, though, her frustration bubbled over. It wasn't like him not to call or text. She checked her phone to make sure, but no apology waited. There was no flirty message promising to meet for breakfast. There was simply ... nothing.

Instead of heading to the tiki bar for a light meal, Rowan went to the employee dining hall. Quinn rarely ate there and this morning looked to be no exception. She forced a smile when she settled at the same table with Sally and focused on her omelet and hash browns.

"You don't look happy," Sally said after a beat, a mug of coffee buffered in her hands. "In fact, you look downright miserable."

Rowan pursed her lips. The last thing she wanted was to start unnecessary ship gossip. Of course, Sally was her best friend on the ship and she needed someone to talk to.

"Quinn never showed up in my room last night."

Sally's expression was hard to read. "Was he supposed to?"

"Well ... we haven't spent a night apart since ... you know. I thought he would eventually show up."

"Did he call?"

Rowan shook her head. "No. I have no idea where he was."

"I know where he was. If you're interested, I mean."

Rowan didn't want to be interested. It wasn't her place to check up on Quinn. Still, she couldn't stop herself from asking the obvious question. "Where was he?"

"He was in the main dining room with Anthony Lowell and that hot diving chick for the entire night," Sally replied. "The bulk of the security team ended up there while the divers had fun at the tiki bar. They drank until well after three in the morning."

Rowan was flummoxed. "He stayed up there drinking all night?"

"I got a report from one of the servers this morning," Sally explained. "She wanted the morning off because she was up so late waiting on them."

"I guess that makes sense."

"I gave her the morning off but I asked for a full report first," Sally supplied. "She said there was a lot of boasting about military operations. She said there was a lot of talk about romancing women from different countries. She also said Quinn was in the middle of it."

The explanation didn't make Rowan feel better. If anything, it made her feel worse. Still, she felt the desperate need to cover. "Well, at least he enjoyed himself." Rowan moved around her breakfast with her fork before pushing the plate away. She'd lost her appetite. "I should probably get to work. We've got a full day of sailing today and if I'm going to take photos of the diving crew enjoying themselves before they get to work, it has to be this afternoon."

Sally rested her hand on Rowan's as a form of solace. "I'm sure he didn't mean for it to happen. When you're drinking, time gets away from you."

"I'm sure he didn't mean it, too." The smile Rowan forced was almost grotesque. "I really do have to get to work, though."

"Okay, well ... if I see Quinn, do you want me to tell him that you're looking for him?"

Rowan's eyes flashed with something akin to fury. "Absolutely not."

Sally chuckled. "You go, girl. Make him pay for forgetting you."

Rowan knew Sally meant it as a joke but being forgotten was one of her biggest fears. "It's not that," she lied. "I simply don't want to take him away from his job."

Sally recognized the statement as a lie but didn't push further. "Well, if you need me, I'll be in the kitchen most of the day."

"Thanks for the offer, but I have other things to focus on." Rowan squared her shoulders, determination washing over her. "I have a job to do, too, right?"

Sally bobbed her head. "Right."

"I'd better go do it."

QUINN WOKE LATE, his head pounding.

At first he thought he was sick, although he rarely fell victim to illness – his immune system was strong, after all – but when he rolled to his side to slide his arm around Rowan and get some comfort he found the other side of the bed empty.

That's when the events of the previous night came flooding back to him and he bolted to a sitting position.

"Oh, geez." He slapped his hand to his forehead, miserable.

Quinn moved slowly as he got ready, downing a handful of aspirin before climbing in the shower and letting the hot water beat down on him for what felt like forever. By the time he hit the tiki bar for breakfast, he was feeling half human ... but just barely. He expected to find Rowan at their regular table, but she wasn't there.

"Where's Rowan?" Quinn asked when Demarcus shoved a mug of coffee in his direction.

"I haven't seen her this morning," Demarcus replied. The bar was empty, which was one of the reasons Quinn and Rowan enjoyed having breakfast there on a regular basis, so the two men could talk freely.

"She wasn't with me when I woke," Quinn noted. "She must've got up early ... although I have no idea why."

Demarcus stared at Quinn for a long beat. "She didn't sleep with you last night."

"What do you mean?" Quinn broke off a piece of the doughnut Demarcus slid in front of him and dunked it in his coffee. "Of course she slept with me."

"Really? How do you think that happened?" Demarcus was well versed in ship gossip. "She waited up here for you for several hours – even though she looked really unhappy when you didn't show, mind you – and then she went to her cabin. Unless you woke alone in her cabin, I can guarantee you two didn't sleep together."

"But ... ." Quinn scrubbed his hand over his cheek to encourage wakefulness. "That's not right."

"I didn't think it was right either. She kept looking at her phone for a message ... and staring at the door you would've come through if you joined her ... and I felt a little sorry for her when she finally gave up and left."

Quinn's stomach jolted at the words. "No ... ."

"Yes." Demarcus bobbed his head. "She waited a long time. Truth be told, though, she looked upset long before you were late. Something was clearly bothering her."

Quinn didn't like the sound of that at all. "Did you talk to her? Did you ask what was wrong?"

"Of course I did. I'm a gossip. I always ask what's wrong. She wouldn't answer. She kept saying nothing was wrong, but I could still tell something was eating at her."

Quinn felt sick to his stomach. "I didn't mean to ... do that."

"Forget about her?"

"I didn't forget about her," Quinn barked, guilt rolling through him. "I could never forget about her. I kept telling Anthony that I had to go, but he wanted me to have a drink with him."

"And I'm guessing one drink turned into ten if your pallor is any indication," Demarcus noted.

"I didn't mean for it to happen," Quinn stressed. "I just ... we were telling stories about Afghanistan and I hadn't been around military folk for a bit. I lost track of time."

"Yes, well, Rowan didn't." Demarcus wasn't trying to hurt Quinn, but he wasn't about to let him off the hook either. "She didn't come here for breakfast. I'm assuming she was ticked when she woke up alone and ate somewhere she wouldn't risk running into you."

Quinn didn't want to believe that, but he was fairly certain Demarcus was right. "I'll find her. I'll fix things."

"I hope so. You guys are cute together. More importantly, I think you're good for one another."

"I'll fix things," Quinn repeated. "I didn't mean for this to happen."

He looked so stricken that Demarcus could barely tamp down the pity rising in his chest. "I'd start on the deck ... but I'd eat something first. You need to look a little less rough around the edges if you expect to use your looks to woo her back."

Quinn bit back a hot retort. "I'll have another doughnut and more coffee."

"There you go." Demarcus beamed. "You also might want to stop in one of the gift shops and get some flowers."

"I've got it under control."

"Yeah, I don't think you do, but it's going to be fun to watch all the same."

ROWAN SPENT **THE MORNING** taking photographs, edging her way around the deck and snapping candid pictures to upload to the ship's internet portal. She doubted very much that anyone would want them, but at least she could say she was doing her job.

The leading edge of her anger with Quinn didn't fade as she

worked, although she managed to push it aside when she caught sight of Nick and Michael. She snapped a bevy of photographs of the two men, quickly shifting her attention to the individuals gathered on the deck when they happened to glance in her direction, and by the time lunch rolled around Rowan had hundreds of photographs to sort through.

She also had a decision to make.

Quinn and Rowan often ate lunch together, either visiting the tiki bar or meeting in the main dining room. Since Rowan wasn't keen to run into Quinn – she was afraid she would embarrass herself and start crying – she picked up a sandwich from one of the small umbrella sellers and picked a spot on the deck to sort through her photos so she wouldn't risk an uncomfortable meeting.

The exact opposite happened.

"Hey." Quinn's voice was low as he approached her.

Rowan jerked her head in his direction, fire filling her eyes before she managed to rein in her fury. "Hello."

She was stiff and formal, something Quinn didn't like.

"Listen, I am so sorry about last night," Quinn offered. "I didn't mean to ... ."

"Forget me?"

"I didn't forget you." Quinn hated her frigid tone. On a normal day she was happy to see him whenever and wherever they could steal a few moments. Now she seemed agitated and eager for him to leave. "I could never forget you."

"And yet you did." Rowan ran her tongue over her lips as she focused on her computer screen. "You completely forgot about me ... as if I didn't even exist."

"Rowan, that is not true." Quinn struggled to maintain his temper. He knew very well that snapping at her when he was in the wrong was the worst possible way to go. "I lost track of time."

"I heard." Rowan clicked on several photos and moved them into the computer's trash bin. "You were up late telling Afghanistan stories with your buddies. Classified Afghanistan stories, I might add.

Ones you couldn't tell in front of me but had no problem telling in front of Andrea Morgan, mind you."

Quinn stilled, dumbfounded. "Are you angry because I didn't make it to the tiki bar or because I told Afghanistan stories?"

"I'm not angry." Rowan's tone was clipped, indicating the exact opposite. "Why would I possibly be angry?"

"Because I said I would meet you at the tiki bar."

"And you didn't. It's hardly the end of the world." Rowan was determined to keep the conversation from turning into a fight. She didn't want to argue in front of The Bounding Storm's crew members – or the divers and other guests, for that matter – so she forced herself to focus on the computer screen.

"Rowan ... ."

"I'm busy right now," Rowan snapped. "I have work to do."

Quinn's guts twisted. "Ro, I'm sorry."

"You don't need to be sorry." Rowan pressed her lips together when she recognized a familiar symbol on one of the photographs, her anger with Quinn falling by the wayside as she leaned forward and stared at the photo.

"I don't think you believe that," Quinn pressed.

"It doesn't really matter what I believe." Rowan clicked another photo featuring the same woman. The symbol was there, signifying death was close and on the hunt. Unfortunately for Rowan, she had no idea who the woman was.

Under different circumstances Rowan would chat about the occurrence with Quinn. They would make a plan to find the woman and do their best to keep her from dying. Now, though, the last thing Rowan wanted to do was spend more time with Quinn. She would have to find out who the woman was on her own.

Rowan snapped her computer shut and flicked her eyes to Quinn, agitation swiftly returning. "I have work to do."

"Rowan, we have to talk about this." Quinn was firm. "I'm am sorry for what happened. I can't fix it if you shut me out, though."

"There's nothing to fix." Rowan was blasé as she cradled the computer to her chest. "You forgot about me. It's over and done with."

"Don't say that." Quinn grabbed Rowan's wrist to still her. "I didn't forget about you. I simply ... lost track of time." The excuse sounded lamer each time he uttered it.

"It's the same thing, Quinn." Rowan carefully extracted her arm. "I have work to do. I believe you do, too." She inclined her chin to a spot over Quinn's shoulder, to where Anthony and Andrea stood and gestured for him. "I believe your friends want to see you."

Quinn was caught. He knew it. More importantly, he knew Rowan recognized it, too. "Rowan, we're not done talking about this."

"There's nothing to talk about." Rowan was breezy as she stepped away from the table. "You forgot about me. You can't take it back. It's done."

"But ... ."

"I have someplace else to be. I'll ... talk to you later, I guess."

She sounded so uncertain that Quinn couldn't fight off the wave of guilt washing over him. He let her go all the same. He knew better than making a scene.

"We're definitely going to talk about this later."

ROWAN WAS STILL RATTLED by her run in with Quinn when she found Sally in the kitchen. The gregarious blonde was holding court, telling some hilarious story about the first time she went diving, when she realized Rowan was not only present but needed attention.

"What's up?"

Rowan led Sally to a corner of the kitchen where they couldn't be overheard and opened her laptop. "I need to find out who this is." She pointed to the woman with the omen hanging over her. Since Sally wasn't aware of Rowan's ability, she didn't question the symbol. To her it was merely part of the background. "Can you think of a way for me to do that?"

"I recognize her," Sally said after a beat. "She's one of the divers. You could ask that Andrea woman. You met her last night, right?"

Rowan nodded, grim. That wasn't her first choice. She was hoping Sally would have a better idea. "Can you think of another way?"

Sally shrugged, unsure. "Maybe." She snapped her fingers to get one of her waitress's attention. "Laura, can you come over here, please?"

The amiable waitress did as she was asked and shuffled over. "What's up?"

"You waited on a lot of the divers last night," Sally said. "Do you recognize this one?"

Laura studied the photo for a long beat and then nodded. "Selena Dennis. I remember because I liked her name. She's part of the elite diving team. I don't know much beyond that. They were good tippers, though."

"Thanks." Sally shooed Laura away before turning back to Rowan. "Does that help?"

Rowan beamed. It was the first genuine smile she'd been able to muster all day. "It helps a great deal. You have no idea how much. Thanks."

Sally grabbed Rowan's wrist before the woman could walk away. "Did you talk to Quinn?"

"There's nothing to talk about."

"I think you're deluding yourself."

"How?" Rowan challenged. "He forgot about me. You said it earlier and I didn't want to admit you were right, but that's exactly what happened. He forgot about me."

"It was an accident. He didn't mean it."

"No, probably not," Rowan agreed. "It's not the first time I've been forgotten, though. It's not the first time I was left to wait for a really long time. It's also not the first time I waited in vain."

"You're talking about your father." Sally felt uneasy. "That was a different situation."

"And yet the outcome was the same," Rowan pointed out. "Neither one of them showed up. It's fine. I'm over it."

Sally knew that was pretty far from the truth. "Rowan ... ."

"I have something I need to do." Rowan kept her smile in place for Sally's benefit. "Thank you for helping me. I'll let you get back to work."

SEVEN

"There he is."

Anthony's voice was booming when he caught sight of Quinn.

"I'm surprised you're up and around," Andrea offered. She wore a slinky bikini, one that showed off her firm assets to perfection, and beamed at Quinn. "I thought you might call in sick today."

Quinn was mildly embarrassed to realize they thought he was a party animal, but he was more troubled by his alienation from Rowan than anything else. "I bounce back pretty quickly."

"Do you feel okay?" Anthony's eyes were full of concern.

"I feel fine," Quinn replied. "What are you guys doing this afternoon?"

"We thought we would wrangle you into hanging out with us at the tiki bar," Andrea said. "Since we don't technically start work until tomorrow, we figured we might as well have some fun today."

Quinn kept his smile in place but offered up a rueful shrug. "I'm on duty. You guys can have some fun, though. That sounds like a good idea to me."

"We can't have fun without you," Anthony countered. "You have the best stories."

"You definitely do," Andrea agreed. "I'm sure we could talk to your boss and get him to let you off the hook."

Quinn pictured Rowan's face when he found her on the deck and immediately started shaking his head. "I honestly have things that require my attention before tomorrow. I need the time."

"Are you sure?" Anthony looked disappointed.

"I'm completely sure," Quinn replied.

"Okay, well, I was hoping you would bring that pretty girlfriend of yours around so she could comment on my size again." Anthony winked in a playful manner. "I haven't seen her at all today and I'm really starting to miss her."

"You're not the only one," Quinn grumbled.

"What did you say?" Andrea was curious.

"Nothing," Quinn replied hurriedly. "I was just talking to myself. As for Rowan, I believe she's taking photographs around the deck. She's busy."

"I saw her about an hour ago," Andrea offered. "She seemed tired or something, maybe a little upset. She was snapping photographs of my divers. I think she's wasting her time because no one is going to buy them, but I suppose she has to prove her worth somehow."

Quinn scowled. "She doesn't have to prove her worth to you. In fact ... ."

Andrea held her hand up to cut him off. "That wasn't a dig. I was talking about the ship owners. It's obvious you find her worthwhile."

"Except you kind of dumped her last night, didn't you?" Anthony furrowed his brow. "I forgot all about her when we started drinking. Did she ever come back around? I'm trying to remember."

"I don't think so," Andrea replied. "We didn't stop until it was almost three. I'm sure that was well past her bedtime."

Quinn didn't like Andrea's derogatory tone but there was little he could do about it. "Yes, well, I have some work to get to. I'm sure we'll sit down and have another discussion before any artifacts are brought up. My main concern today is handling the security around the salon.

I'll get in touch with you by the end of the day about security badges."

Anthony flashed an enthusiastic thumbs-up. "It sounds like a plan."

"Great."

QUINN WAS STILL FEELING guilty and annoyed two hours later as he walked through the salon for what he hoped would be the last time that afternoon. He'd checked all the doors, tested the scanners himself, and then opted for one final walk through.

That's where Sally found him.

"You scared the bejeesus out of me," Quinn complained when he saw her. "I thought I was in here alone."

"Obviously not," Sally said dryly.

"So much for my security."

"I happen to know Julio, who you have on the front door," Sally pointed out. "I threatened not to feed him if he didn't let me in. I think he's more afraid of my wrath than yours."

Quinn scowled. "Probably. What else is new?"

"Quite a bit actually." Sally kept her shoulders squared as she sat on the bench at the edge of the room. "I had breakfast with Rowan this morning."

Quinn's stomach flipped as he regarded the normally gregarious woman. She was somewhat muted, and he didn't like it one bit. "I saw her on the deck."

"Did you?" Sally cocked an eyebrow. "Did you apologize?"

"Yes."

"Did she accept it?"

"No."

"See, I knew that." Sally rested her hands on her knees as she cracked her neck. "Do you want to know how?"

"I sincerely doubt it."

"I try to make a point of staying out of your relationship, Quinn," Sally offered. "I'm not sure I can do that this go around."

"You try to make a point of staying out of our relationship?" Quinn was flabbergasted. "Since when?"

"Um ... every day since you got together."

"You're full of so much crap I'm afraid to flush because I'm sure I'll clog the toilet line."

Sally's frown was pronounced. "Listen, I like to gossip as much as the next person, but that doesn't mean I involve myself in your relationship. Did I smack you upside the head when you didn't make a move on Rowan right away? No. Did I get involved when you guys weren't having sex for what felt like forever? No."

"You basically did both those things," Quinn argued.

"You're remembering it wrong." Sally was succinct. "This time I can't stay out of it, though. This time I have to get involved."

"Oh, I'm going to hate this, aren't I?" Quinn pressed the heel of his hand to his forehead. "Go ahead and tell me ... although, do it gently. I'm not sure how much more I can take."

"And people say I'm dramatic."

"You are."

"Yes, well, it's going to get worse." Sally scratched the side of her nose as she pinned Quinn with a hard look. "You broke her heart."

Whatever he was expecting, that wasn't it. Quinn openly gaped. Sally, though, she remained calm, refusing to scream and yell at him even though he would've been far more comfortable with the effort. "What do you mean?"

"You broke her heart, Quinn," Sally repeated. "It might seem ludicrous to us – and I tried to talk her down a few hours ago only to have her hurry away so she wouldn't have to listen to me – but it's rational to her."

"It's going to be okay." Quinn was almost a hundred percent sure of that. "I'm going to get away from everyone, talk to her alone, and apologize. Everything will be back to normal in a few hours."

"See, I don't think that's true," Sally said. "That's why I felt the need to come to you. She's really upset."

"I didn't mean for it to happen," Quinn supplied. "I just lost track of time."

"You forgot her."

"Stop saying that." Quinn extended a warning finger. "I did not forget her. It's just ... they wanted to have one drink. I thought I could extricate myself after that. I'm head of security and I'm supposed to work with these people so I couldn't simply walk away when they wanted to talk."

"Are you trying to convince me or yourself?" Sally asked dryly.

"I'm merely stating the truth."

"So ... yourself then?"

Quinn made an odd growling noise. "What do you want, Sally?"

"To make sure you fix this."

"Fix her broken heart?"

"Don't sound so incredulous," Sally chided. "You're not looking at it the same way she is."

"And what way is that?" Quinn challenged.

"First, stop giving me attitude," Sally ordered. "I didn't create this mess. You did. You should've seen her face when she finally realized you weren't coming last night. It was ... ridiculous. She kept looking toward the door at every noise. She thought she would see you there. When she realized you weren't coming ... ."

"Don't finish that sentence." Quinn already felt guilty. He didn't need Sally adding to the mix. "I didn't mean for it to happen. Time and drinks got away from me."

"I get that. I really do. If I were the one you stood up, I would've punished you for a few hours – made you give me massages and flowers and stuff – and then forgiven you as long as the kisses kept coming and I felt you were really sorry. She saw things from a slightly different perspective."

"And what perspective is that?"

"She saw them from the perspective of a teenage girl who came home one day to wait for her father. He never showed up either."

Quinn felt as if he'd been punched in the stomach ... with a bag of bricks. "Oh, I didn't even think about that." He rested his hand on the back of the bench. "Of course she would be reminded of that."

"She doesn't talk about that a lot to me," Sally noted. "Does she talk about it with you?"

"A little."

"She's still haunted by a father who never came home. I know it's not the same – or even remotely the same, for that matter – as what happened last night. I think it's fair to say she has abandonment issues, though."

"I should've realized." Quinn felt even guiltier than before, if that was possible. "I should've walked away before they even offered me a drink."

"Listen, don't beat yourself up too much," Sally admonished. "Nobody is perfect – not you, not me, and not Rowan – but it will probably benefit you to realize what she's dealing with."

"I need to talk to her." Quinn rolled his neck. "I don't like this hanging over my head."

"I don't think she likes it either. She's been acting a bit ... odd."

Quinn stilled, surprised. "Odd how?"

"I think she's focusing on work because it's the only way she can push her worry and doubts out of her head."

"Meaning?"

"Meaning she's become obsessive about one of the guests."

"I'm going to need more information," Quinn prodded. "And, if you tell me it's a man, I might be the one with a broken heart."

Sally snorted. "It's a woman. Her name is Selena Dennis. She's part of Andrea Morgan's elite diving team."

Quinn was confused. "And Rowan is suddenly obsessed with her?"

"She brought me a photo and showed it to me, asked if I could think of a way to find out who the woman was without making a big deal out of it. I told her to ask Andrea, but she declined. I think she's feeling a little bit insecure because you spent the entire night with Andrea."

"I didn't spend the night with Andrea," Quinn countered. "I spent it with Anthony."

Sally quirked an eyebrow. "I'm not sure that's much better."

Quinn scowled. "Go back to the photo. Did Rowan say why she wanted to know about the woman?"

Sally shook her head. "She just said she wanted to know who the woman was. One of my waitresses recognized her, told her the name, and then Rowan couldn't get out of there fast enough."

"But ... why?" Quinn asked the question, but he figured out the answer on his own before Sally could provide her opinion. In truth, no matter how she tried, Sally couldn't come up with the right answer because she didn't know about Rowan's ability. Quinn, on the other hand, knew all about it. "Son of a ... ."

"Do you know what she wants with Selena Dennis?" Sally was understandably intrigued.

"No, but I've got a pretty good idea." Quinn strode toward the door. "Thanks for giving me a heads-up, Sally. I'll take it from here."

"Try not to yell at her," Sally called out. "Insecurity is a pain in the keister, but Rowan comes by it honestly. The biggest part of her heart believes that her father died that day and they simply never found his body. A small part, one that refuses to completely let go, believes he purposely abandoned her because she wasn't worthy. She just can't get over that no matter how much you want her to."

Quinn paused, his fingers wrapped around the door handle. "I'm not angry with her."

"You seem angry."

"I'm angry with myself. I'll fix this, though. I promise."

"Good luck."

"Thanks. I think I'm going to need it."

ROWAN'S STOMACH GROWLED as she sat on the deck and watched Selena Dennis sip a piña colada and chat with several friends. The woman looked happy, relaxed even. That didn't mean she would stay that way.

Rowan kept her camera at the ready and snapped another photograph, frowning as she pulled back and stared at the image in the electronic viewfinder on the device's back. The symbol would come and go from older photos as danger waxed and waned but Rowan wasn't convinced it was always accurate so she insisted on snapping new photos whenever possible. It was a habit she couldn't shake.

"You don't look happy."

Rowan jolted at the new voice, sliding a sideways glance to a smiling Nick as he moved closer. "I was concentrating."

"You look like you were concentrating hard."

"Yes, well, I can't seem to help myself when it comes to my job." The smile Rowan let loose with was full of faux sugar and light. "I haven't seen much of you today. Have you been hiding?"

Nick snorted. "Why would I hide? I've been busy coming up with an action plan for the dive site. If I knew you were looking for me, though, I would've made my presence known."

He had a smarmy quality that Rowan wasn't completely comfortable with. She didn't retreat, though, instead fixing him with a weighted look. "And here I thought you were avoiding me after you mentioned knowing about my past. I guess that was silly, huh?"

Nick didn't look happy with the conversational shift, but he didn't run away. "I double checked your file and there was a notation in it about your circumstances as a teenager. That's how I knew."

Rowan didn't believe him for a second. "Well, I guess that explains everything ... including why I feel as if I should know you."

Nick's eyes were clear as they locked with hers. "I guess I just have one of those faces."

"Yeah, I guess." Rowan licked her lips before turning her attention back to Selena. "What can you tell me about her?"

"Selena?" Nick arched an eyebrow. "Why do you want to know?"

Rowan shrugged, noncommittal. "A few of the waitresses were talking about her," she lied. "They said she was a real party animal." Rowan was playing a hunch, but she wasn't worried about Nick calling her on it. He seemed too wrapped up in his own games to care about the ones Rowan wanted to play.

"I don't know if I would call her a party animal," Nick hedged. "She likes to hang out with friends, but when it comes to work, she's very good at what she does."

"And she's part of the elite dive team, right? What exactly does that mean?"

"She'll be with the first group that goes down." Nick's expression was thoughtful. "Why are you interested in that? You're not a diver, right? Why do you care?"

"I guess I'm just curious." Rowan pursed her lips as she raised her camera and snapped three shots in rapid succession. She stared at the viewfinder again, her stomach refusing to unclench. "How dangerous is the initial dive?"

"I don't know." Nick's response was slow, deliberate. "Why do you ask?"

"I'm just curious. I'm curious about the entire thing."

"You seem the curious sort," Nick agreed. "I don't know what to tell you about Selena. I am curious why you're so interested in her, though."

"I'm merely interested in the job," Rowan corrected. "As for the rest ... I was merely asking questions."

"Yes, well ... ." Nick didn't get a chance to finish because his attention was diverted by an approaching Quinn. "Ah, here comes your paramour. Perhaps he'll know why you're so interested in Ms. Dennis."

Rowan cringed when she heard Quinn's footsteps on the deck behind her. "Well, great."

"Mr. Davenport, it's good to see you." Nick beamed. "How are you this afternoon?"

"I'm good, Mr. Green," Quinn replied, his voice even.

"Would you care to join us?" Nick asked. "We were just having an illuminating discussion."

"Actually, I was hoping to have a private discussion with Ms. Gray." Quinn managed to keep his wits and manners on display, but just barely. "You don't mind, do you?"

"Of course not." Nick held up his hands as he took a step back. "I'll leave you to your discussion."

"Great." Quinn remained where he was, his eyes focused on Rowan's face until he was sure they were alone. The second Nick made his escape, Rowan looked as if that was exactly what she wanted to do. There was no way Quinn was going to allow that to happen.

"I should probably get going," Rowan said lamely, hating the fact that she felt so uncomfortable in Quinn's presence.

"Oh, you're not going anywhere," Quinn countered. "In fact, if you try leaving, I'm going to cuff you to me until we work this out."

"Is that a threat?"

"Nope. It's a promise. We need to talk, and we're going to do it right now. I won't wait another second ... and I honestly don't think you want me to."

Rowan considered arguing but she was too tired and defeated to muster the energy. "Fine. I'm furious, though. You should prepare yourself."

Despite his worry, Quinn's lips quirked. "Right back at you."

EIGHT

"Fine. What do you want to talk about?"

"Don't take that tone with me." Quinn was firm as he tugged Rowan toward a set of chairs near the edge of the deck. That section of the boat was empty, which meant they could talk without fear of being overheard. "I know you're upset, but we're going to work through this right now."

Rowan heaved out a long-suffering sigh as she sank into one of the chairs, lifting her camera to study a photo before turning her full attention to Quinn. "I'm not upset."

"Okay, don't lie." Quinn took the chair next to her and fixed her with a determined look. "I don't like how flippant you sound."

"How do you want me to sound?"

"Like my Rowan."

He was so earnest Rowan wanted to melt right there, but she held firm. "Your Rowan?"

"Yeah, that's how I think of you."

"You didn't last night."

"That's not true," Quinn protested. "I had every intention of meeting you at the tiki bar. Things got away from me."

"I heard."

Quinn struggled to maintain his temper. He'd never seen Rowan so purposely blasé. It irritated him to his very core. "I didn't mean for it to happen. It was an accident. That doesn't make it right, though. I'm very sorry."

"You don't have to be sorry."

"But I am." Quinn grabbed three fingers on her left hand so she couldn't pull too far away. "It wasn't on purpose. I had every intention of getting out of there right away, but Anthony wanted to talk about the salon setup and I didn't feel as if I could simply take off.

"This isn't an excuse, mind you, but I thought you would want to know the way it went down," he continued. "I agreed to sketch out the layout for him and he insisted I have a beer. I wasn't really in the mood, but I did it anyway."

"Ah, peer pressure," Rowan lamented. "If only you weren't so susceptible to doing what the other cool kids are doing."

Quinn frowned. "I guess that's fair, although I really wish you wouldn't act so cold and just come out with what's bothering you."

"Nothing is bothering me."

"Ugh. You're going to be the death of me." Quinn rolled his neck and stared at the setting sun before continuing. "We talked a bit about Afghanistan and traded stories. One beer turned into several beers. I lost my head."

"I'm not your keeper, Quinn. You don't have to explain yourself to me."

"I do. I said I would be at the tiki bar in a few minutes and it didn't happen. I am so sorry. I don't even know if I can express how sorry I am."

Part of Rowan wanted to take pity on him, but she tamped down the urge. "It's fine. Don't worry about it." She averted her gaze. "I should probably get inside and upload these photos."

"Oh, we're nowhere near being done," Quinn said. "I made a big mistake. I should've walked away before the beer started flowing. I need you to know that I am sorry, though. I didn't mean for it to happen ... and I certainly didn't mean to hurt you. That's the last thing I wanted."

"I don't want you to be forced to spend time with me when you don't want to do it," Rowan supplied. "That's not the kind of relationship I want."

"That's not the kind of relationship I want either. That's not what happened, though. I simply ... lost track of time. It was like being in the military again. People were sharing stories ... and it was a brotherhood of sorts ... but that doesn't explain away what I did. I can't go back in time and fix it, though. All I can do is apologize."

Rowan swallowed hard. "You should've texted. That would've been enough."

"I know, and I'm sorry for that, too. I swear it won't happen again."

"I don't want you to think of me as your mother."

Quinn cracked a smile. "I can guarantee that's not how I think of you."

"Okay." Rowan held up her free hand in surrender. "It's fine. I accept your apology."

She said the words he longed to hear, but Quinn couldn't leave things how they were. They weren't in sync yet. Not even close.

"You're still hurt and I know why." Quinn kept his voice low as he squeezed the fingers he held. "You were abandoned as a teenager and you can't help equating what I did last night to what happened when you were eighteen."

"I don't know that I was abandoned. I might've been orphaned. Heck, I probably was orphaned."

"Probably," Quinn conceded. "That doesn't change the fact that you can't get over the idea that you might've been abandoned. It's okay, Ro. I get it. I didn't mean to stir all this up."

Rowan opened her mouth to respond, but no sound came out so she snapped it shut.

"What were you going to say?" Quinn prodded.

"I honestly don't know. On one hand, I feel pathetic for forcing a situation where those two things are even close to being equal. They're not, for the record. You simply forgot about me and got drunk. It's not close to the same thing as what happened when I was younger."

"I didn't forget about you, Ro." Quinn leaned forward and placed his head in front of her face so she would have no choice but to meet his gaze. "I swear I didn't. I lost track of time and then I got drunk. I could never forget about you. Things simply got away from me and I'm sorry."

"You don't have to keep apologizing."

"I'm going to do it until I'm sure you've forgiven me."

"I'm not angry."

Quinn arched a challenging eyebrow. "Say that again without twisting your lips the way you just did."

"I'm not angry," Rowan repeated. She meant it. "I'm just ... tired and cranky. I didn't sleep well and I've had a long day. You don't have to keep apologizing, though. It's not as if you've been wandering around kicking puppies or anything."

"No, but looking at your face this afternoon made me feel as if I'd done exactly that."

Rowan wrinkled her nose. "Are you equating me to a dog in that scenario?"

Quinn's grin was quick and easy. "They're man's best friend for a reason."

"Well ... woof."

Quinn took them both by surprise when he swooped in and kissed her. The exchange wasn't passionate, or even desperate. It was merely simple ... and needed. He tucked a strand of hair behind her ear when he pulled back.

"I'll never just take off like that again," he promised. "That wasn't fair to you and I should've realized how you would take it."

"You shouldn't have to treat me differently than you would anyone else," Rowan countered. "I'm not special. There's no reason for me to act as if I'm falling apart simply because you forgot about me."

"Okay, if you say that again, I'm going to wrestle you to the deck and tickle you until you promise to never use that word again," Quinn warned. "As for the rest ... you are special. You're special in so many ways I don't know where to start listing them."

"Yeah?"

Quinn nodded. "You have no idea. Sometimes you're frustratingly oblivious to your own appeal. I don't get it ... and sometimes find it irritating ... but there it is."

"I still acted like a baby."

"No, you acted like the wronged party. You had every right to be angry. What I did was ... all kinds of rude. The thing is, I didn't want to stay with them. All I could think about was getting to you at the tiki bar. It was as if they didn't want me to go and worked overtime to keep me with them."

"Maybe Andrea has a crush on you."

Quinn didn't bother to hide his amusement. "I doubt it. If she has a crush on anyone, it's Anthony. I think he has a crush on you, by the way. He asked about you this afternoon. They wanted me to drink with them again."

Rowan was taken aback. "Who drinks that much?"

Quinn smirked. "We drank that much when I was overseas. I don't think it's out of the ordinary. I am starting to think that Sally and Demarcus are right when they say we're a bit staid, though.

"You and I are the types of people who are perfectly happy with a book and a mug of hot chocolate," he continued. "I was always that way before my tour, but I got away from myself a bit overseas. When I came back, I reverted. I guess I reverted a bit in the other direction last night."

"And I should've considered that," Rowan noted. "I didn't want to keep you from them. I didn't realize that maybe it was important for you to hang out with them."

"It wasn't important. Trust me. When I woke up with the world's worst hangover this morning, I remembered exactly why I hated that life."

Rowan pressed her lips together to keep from laughing. "Were you in pain?"

"Yes."

"Is it wrong that I feel a bit better because of that?"

Quinn snickered. "No. I consider it my punishment, too. Do you know what my greatest regret was, though?"

"Did you have cotton mouth?"

Quinn shook his head. "I was alone in my bed. I didn't have you."

Whatever resentment she was holding onto melted with his words. "Wow, you sure know how to end an argument, huh?"

Quinn's expression was rueful. "I certainly hope so." He leaned forward, cupping the back of her head as he rested his forehead against hers. "I am sorry. It won't happen again."

"Okay." Rowan heaved out a sigh. "Everything is okay."

"Good." Quinn pressed another kiss to Rowan's mouth, this one more intense and needy. Rowan returned it in kind, sinking into him as he slipped his arm around her waist and tugged her so she shared his chair. He leaned back, stroking the back of her head as they melted together. After a few minutes, he was reluctant to pull away, but the sound of Rowan's growling stomach made him realize they couldn't disappear into each other for the entire night. "Better?"

Rowan bit her bottom lip and nodded.

"Good." Quinn wrapped his arms around her, sighing when she rested her chin on his chest as he leaned back in the chair.

"I'm officially hungry," Rowan announced, causing Quinn to chuckle.

"I know. I heard your stomach."

"Let's go eat."

"We will. We're not quite done talking about the fight yet."

This time the look on Rowan's face was full of confusion. "We're not?"

"I believe you need to tell me about Selena Dennis, don't you?"

"Oh." Rowan knit her eyebrows. "How do you even know about her?"

"Sally has a big mouth and a few opinions that she's unwilling to keep to herself," Quinn replied. "She thought you were focusing on Selena because you were desperate for a distraction, but I knew straight away what you were really doing."

Rowan held up her camera so Quinn could look at the viewfinder.

"She's got the omen," Quinn said after a beat. "Did she have it yesterday?"

Rowan shrugged. "I didn't take any photos of her yesterday. I went back to look but there was nothing to look at. This trip is different so I haven't been going out of my way to take photographs of everyone."

"Which makes sense." Quinn rolled his neck as he prodded Rowan to cuddle closer. "Don't pull away yet. I want you close while we think through our problem."

"Just so you know, this is not us making up. I want to make up when we're alone and in my quarters later. Or your quarters. I don't care which quarters. I'm not picky."

Quinn chuckled as he absently rubbed her back. "I have that on my agenda, too. It's right after I feed you and right before we take a long bath in the private high-roller Jacuzzi."

Rowan stilled, dumbfounded. "We can do that?"

"We're *going* to do that," Quinn clarified. "I happen to have a key card that allows me to lock the door, and that's exactly what we're going to do tonight. Besides, there are only two people on the ship who have key cards for that area. What are the odds they'll try to make a visit tonight?"

"I don't know. I can't think now that you've mentioned the Jacuzzi."

Quinn grinned. "We have to deal with the Selena situation first. We'll definitely get to the Jacuzzi, though. What have you found out about Selena? I know you've been asking questions about her all afternoon."

"Not a lot. I didn't want to draw too much attention to myself. I mostly just followed her around."

"But?"

"But she's with the elite diving team," Rowan replied. "From what I understand, that means she's going to be with the first team that hits the site."

"That could be dangerous simply because it's the first group. Anthony said the water in that area is known for being treacherous and the entire team is worried about pirates swooping in and attacking."

"Is it wrong that my head just went to a Johnny Depp place?"

"Not if that puts you in a good mood." Quinn brushed his lips against Rowan's forehead, thankful beyond measure that she'd forgiven him and they seemed to be back on track. "Did you talk to Selena at all?"

"I tried, but you know how bad I am at talking to people when I'm trying to figure out how they're going to die. I kind of turn into a total geek ... kind of like you with the history books."

"Ha, ha." Quinn poked her belly before sobering. "I don't know what to do about this situation. We dock tomorrow, and after that we'll be operating from a stationary position. That's pretty much the opposite of what we've dealt with prior to this."

"You're assuming that she's going to die in the water by the site," Rowan pointed out. "What if she's going to die on the ship? What if it's supposed to happen before we dock? What if it's supposed to happen tonight, in fact?"

Quinn shrugged. "I honestly don't know. I hadn't even considered that."

"Probably because you drank so much liquor last night. You're still slow."

"And you're getting your feisty attitude back." Quinn was

secretly pleased by that development. "Did you find out where her room was located?"

"Funnily enough, they've sort of segregated everyone," Rowan replied, struggling to sit up.

"Not yet." Quinn tugged her back. "I'm not joking. I need you right here for another few minutes. I'm not ready to release you."

"I can't decide if you're being cute or ... something else."

"It's probably a mixture of both, but we won't talk about it after tonight."

"Sure." Rowan tugged on her bottom lip. "So, as for the rooms, since not everything is taken they have the teams spreading out over multiple floors. There are a total of five dive teams with varying degrees of security clearance. Each team has their own section on various decks."

"Give me an example."

"Okay, the elite team – which is the one I paid the closest attention to – has taken over the B deck on level five."

"The entire section?"

"Yeah, they're taking over multiple rooms for each person."

"Okay, I guess that makes sense ... although it seems a bit wasteful. Still, the company funding the dive has money to burn so I guess they're able to do whatever they want."

"Everyone is segregated, including security. It's like cliques in high school. I don't know how else to explain it."

"Hmm." Quinn turned Rowan's head so he could kiss the tender spot behind her ear as she considered what to do next.

"You're making my brain fuzzy," Rowan complained.

"I know. That's part of my plan. Wait until I get you into the Jacuzzi."

"What about Selena, though?" Rowan pressed. "We have to watch her."

"I'll put guards close to her room and have them watch the B-deck cameras. I don't know what else we can do. I don't suppose you know where she is right now, do you?"

Rowan nodded, taking him by surprise. "She's right over there." She pointed toward the deck area closest to the railing and frowned when she realized it was empty. "Okay, she was right there before we decided to have our serious discussion. I don't think she could've gone far."

"Then we'll find her. Give me another kiss first."

"Shouldn't we focus on work?"

"Only if you're trying to torture me."

Rowan gave in and pressed her lips to his. "Better?"

Quinn bobbed his head, his chest warming with happiness. "You have no idea. In fact ... ." He didn't get a chance to finish because an ear-splitting scream filled the air and caused both of them to jump to their feet as they snapped their heads in the direction of the ship's aft.

"Son of a ... I guess we should've seen this coming."

NINE

Rowan and Quinn bolted toward the sound of the screaming, Quinn extending a hand to block Rowan from running ahead – while also keeping her close – as he cocked his head to the side.

"This way." Quinn pointed as he broke into a run, making sure he kept one ear behind him so he didn't lose Rowan. He was keyed up and agitated, and the sight that greeted him once they turned the corner and hit the aft area didn't make him feel any better.

A woman, long brown hair flying, struggled with a hooded figure close to the railing. The man – and it had to be a man because he was too tall to be a woman – worked overtime to push the screaming woman over the railing as she desperately fought to hold him off.

"That's Selena Dennis," Rowan said, pulling up short.

Quinn didn't spare her a glance. He couldn't. He had a situation to handle ... and there was only one way to do it. "Hey!"

He bellowed the words, causing the tall figure to snap his head in their direction.

To Rowan, it was as if time stopped moving. The two men stared each other down – although there was no way to make out the face of the individual threatening Selena because he wore a hoodie to cover his face – and something chilling passed between them. Then, as if a spell had been broken, the man grabbed Selena around the neck and heaved her over the railing.

Rowan's mouth opened as she let loose with a scream, the action serving to break her free from the ice block she momentarily found herself in. Quinn picked up his pace, lowering his head as he skidded toward the end of the ship.

The man bolted in the opposite direction, only looking over his shoulder when he was far enough away to risk it. Quinn took Rowan by surprise when he didn't follow, instead focusing on the railing where Selena went over. Rowan considered giving chase – which would've been a stupid idea – but Quinn's voice caused her to focus on him rather than Selena's assailant.

"Ro, I need you to help me."

It was only then that Rowan realized Quinn had his hands full with Selena. She hadn't gone completely over, instead clinging to the railing from the other side, her eyes wide with terror as her ashen features revealed a woman who realized she was one misstep away from falling to her death.

"I've got him!" Anthony yelled, drawing Rowan's gaze as he broke into a run and started chasing the hooded figure.

Rowan quickly lost track of them as she stepped to Quinn's side and swallowed hard. He had hold of Selena's arm but was at an awkward angle. He flicked a glance to Rowan, grim determination flitting through his eyes. When he spoke, it was with a calm voice that soothed Rowan's fraying nerves.

"Baby, I need to lean pretty far over the railing to grab Selena. That means I need someone to anchor me here."

Rowan nodded as if she understood, but Quinn wasn't sure she did.

"That's you," Quinn said. "You need to hold my legs ... and you need to hold them tight ... because I'm going to be using all my upper body strength to pull Selena over. Do you understand?"

Rowan nodded without hesitation. She was too terrified to argue with him.

Quinn kept hold of Selena's arm as he climbed the railing, positioning himself close to the top before leaning over. Rowan dropped to her knees and wrapped her arms around Quinn's legs, pinning him to the railing as she pressed her face into his calves and closed her eyes. Her grip was so tight Quinn thought there was a chance she would cut off his circulation. He didn't say anything to change her stance, though.

Quinn was determined as he grabbed Selena with both arms. He held her terrified gaze and spoke in a soft tone. "I'm going to pull you over. It's important you don't panic. I won't let go. I promise."

"Just get me up," Selena screeched. "Get me up now!"

Quinn tugged with everything he had and dragged the woman toward the top of the railing. It was smooth sailing until her foot snagged on the top bar. For one brief moment, Quinn thought she might tumble backward, but Selena regrouped and gave one final push, throwing herself at Quinn with such force she caused him to topple over.

Because Rowan held so tightly to his legs and Selena dug her fingers into his neck to make sure she didn't fall, Quinn was in an awkward position when he landed.

"You're okay," Quinn murmured as Selena burst into tears, patting her shoulder in a lame attempt to calm her. "You're okay."

"I almost died," Selena wailed, burrowing her face in his shoulder.

"You didn't, though." Quinn was uncomfortable with Selena's clinging nature, but he couldn't dislodge her given how he was positioned. That meant he had to force Rowan to move, although she seemed to be in her own little world. "Ro, honey ... ."

"I won't let go." Rowan didn't open her eyes and her firm grip caused Quinn to smile despite the fact that he was extremely uncomfortable and Selena's fingernails were digging into the tender skin on the back of his neck.

"You didn't let go, Ro." Quinn took his free hand and pressed it to the back of her head. "I need you to now, though, because I'm in serious pain."

"What?" Rowan lifted her head, realization dawning. "Oh." She jerked back, allowing Quinn to straighten his legs and sigh. "I'm sorry."

"Don't be sorry." Quinn's lips curved. "You did exactly what I asked."

"Yeah." Rowan's chest heaved as she stared at Selena. The woman clung to Quinn, which generally would've been something that bothered her, but she understood fear and Selena was clearly overcome with it so Rowan let it slide. She lifted her eyes to the deck at the sound of footsteps, meeting Anthony's keen gaze as he came to a stop. He was alone, which made her think the chase didn't go well. "You lost him?"

Anthony nodded, frustrated. "He disappeared through an employee door. I couldn't follow."

"Do you know which one?" Quinn was gentle as he tried to dislodge Selena. She was having none of it, though, and only snuggled closer.

"Yeah. I can show you."

"We might get lucky and find something on the cameras." Quinn was firm when he grabbed Selena's wrists this time, dragging them down and pushing her back a bit. "We need to get Selena to medical and then we'll check the cameras and card scanners. It's important we find out who did this."

"Then let's get to it," Anthony said, his eyes alive with excitement. "The faster we find this guy, the faster we can hit the bar tonight."

Quinn lobbed a worried look in Rowan's direction and found her face unreadable. "I want to find who did this, but I'm not going to the bar tonight."

"You're wimping out?" Anthony was appalled. "Why?"

"Let's just say I have something important I want to do with my night and leave it at that. Now ... come on. This might take longer than both of us want."

IN THE END, **THEY** came up with very little to help their investigation. The key card used to access the employee door was stolen from one of the break rooms during an afternoon shift. The cameras caught the suspect entering the hallway but lost him when he turned a corner. The hoodie itself was found discarded in a trash receptacle on the third floor.

They had nothing to track the man in question and were left with more questions than answers.

"I'm exhausted," Rowan said as she sat at the end of the bed upon returning to her room later that night. She groaned as she leaned over to remove her shoes, but Quinn beat her to it, kneeling in front of her and sliding off the belted sandals.

"You didn't have to do that." Rowan was sheepish.

"Maybe I wanted to," Quinn said. "Maybe I wanted to play Cinderella. Did you ever consider that?"

"The prince put the shoe on Cinderella's foot. He didn't take it off."

"Oh, well, I'm much too tired for that." Quinn took her by surprise when he pressed a kiss to the bottom of her foot, causing her to squirm. "Ticklish, huh?"

"Maybe a little." Rowan struggled to a standing position and tugged off her shirt and shorts. They managed to eat, although it wasn't the romantic dinner Quinn envisioned because Anthony and Andrea insisted they all sit together and talk about the attack.

For her part, Selena was sedated and kept in the hospital wing for the night. Quinn put two guards on her to be safe, but he doubted very much anyone would make a second attempt so close to the first failure.

Anthony and Andrea were convinced it had to be some sort of sexual attack – although that made zero sense to Quinn – and they refused to discard the notion. They worked tirelessly to get Quinn to stay with them after dinner, down another few rounds of drinks, but Quinn was adamant when he declined.

Finally, when Anthony saw him slide his arm around Rowan's shoulders and direct her toward the door, he gave up and wished them a pleasant evening. He looked sad to see them go, though, and Quinn couldn't help thinking it was because he wanted Rowan close rather than him. Anthony seemed enamored with the ship photographer, and he had no problem showing it.

"I know I promised to take you to the Jacuzzi tonight, but I think we both need some sleep first," Quinn said. "The good thing is, I have plenty of time to get you there over the next week or so ... and I swear I'm going to do it. I hope you're not too disappointed."

"I'm disappointed, but mostly because we didn't get to spend any time alone. I'm looking forward to the Jacuzzi, but I can wait."

Quinn's smile dipped. "I'm sorry we didn't get any alone time. I wanted that, too."

Rowan waved off the apology. "It's not as if it was your fault. You saved a life. You saved Selena's life."

"*We* saved her life," Quinn corrected. "I'm still sorry. I wanted a quiet night with you more than anything."

"We can still have that." Rowan pointed toward the bed. "It will simply be really quiet."

Quinn chuckled as he stripped out of his shirt and shorts, leaving only his boxer shorts in place as he hit the light and crawled in next to Rowan. "Come here," he murmured as they got comfortable, moving to his side and drawing her back to his chest as he wrapped his arm around her. "I promise to romance the crap out of you as soon as we figure this all out."

Rowan snorted, genuinely amused. "I don't need you to romance the crap out of me. It's nice, don't get me wrong, but I'm perfectly comfortable with this."

Quinn kissed her neck. "I'm still going to do it." He was so tired he knew he would drift off soon. He wanted Rowan to be with him when he did. "I'm going to make this up to you."

"You already have."

"How?"

Rowan linked her fingers with his and pressed his hand to her chest. "You're here."

Quinn's heart pinged at her earnest words. "Oh, I'm definitely going to romance the crap out of you."

"I love it when you phrase it like that."

"Just wait until I start the romance."

THEY SLEPT HARD, both of them tumbling directly into dreamland. When they woke, they were in the exact same positions and cuddled together. Rowan shifted as she stretched, rolling so she could face Quinn as the morning sunshine filtered through the window.

"Morning," Quinn murmured as he pressed a kiss to the tip of her nose. "How did you sleep?"

"Better than I expected," Rowan admitted. "I thought I would have nightmares about what happened – I used to have dreams about falling quite a bit when my father disappeared – but I slept hard. I can't even remember what I dreamed about."

Quinn tucked a strand of Rowan's hair behind her ear. "I used to hang out with a guy when I was overseas who analyzed dreams. He spent all his time doing it. I think he just wanted something to focus on besides his fear. Anyway, he once told me that falling represents insecurity and feelings of being overwhelmed."

"Did you believe him?"

Quinn shrugged. "I think it made sense. I don't want you feeling insecure."

"I'm not sure you can fix that. You're not the person who started the insecurity train. Unless you can find my father and give me answers, I think I'm stuck."

Quinn licked his lips. "If you want, I can look into that."

The offer was simple, straightforward, and yet it caught Rowan off guard. "What?"

"I can look into it," Quinn repeated. "We can even take time together and go back ... if you want, I mean."

Rowan was floored. "You would do that for me?"

"There's very little I wouldn't do for you. I believe all the options involve dancing to rap music in public and voluntarily hanging out with clowns." The lame joke earned him a wan smile so Quinn plowed forward. "If you want me to see if I can figure out what happened to your father, I'm more than willing to do it."

Rowan swallowed hard, the offer touching her in a way she didn't know was possible. "Thank you."

"You're welcome." Quinn kissed her forehead, the effort gentle and yet wrenchingly intimate. "Is that what you want? As soon as this job is over, I can start looking into times that will work."

"I don't know if I want that," Rowan admitted, resting her fingertips on his chest. "I always thought that was what I wanted ... right up until you offered to see if you could find answers."

Quinn instantly understood what she was getting at. "You want to know and yet you're afraid to actually find out."

"I've always thought that not knowing was the worst possible thing." Rowan licked her lips as she scratched the side of her nose. "I'm not sure that's true, though. What if I find out he's dead and lose that last bit of hope in the back of my brain? The part that thinks maybe he got hit over the head and is out there with amnesia."

"Amnesia is pretty rare, Ro."

"I know, but it's still a sliver of hope, isn't it? I also have hope that the government was out to get him – although I have no idea why – and he ran to keep me safe. I dream that he's out there and watches over me whenever he can."

"I get it." And, because he did, Quinn could do nothing but draw her closer. "You don't have to do anything before you're ready. We can leave it for now."

"Thank you."

"We'll revisit this conversation when we're both more settled," Quinn offered. "That's down the road, but I'm sure it will work out."

"Great." Rowan burrowed her face in the hollow of his neck. "Thank you for offering, though."

"The offer stands. When you're ready, we'll talk."

"Okay."

The duo lapsed into amiable silence, both content to remain where they were, until something occurred to Rowan and she snapped her head back. "Oh!"

Quinn reluctantly released her as she scrambled from the bed, taking a moment to enjoy the way she looked in nothing but her sleep tank and panties before furrowing his brow as she returned to the bed with her camera in tow. "What are you doing? I don't know how I feel about taking dirty selfies."

Rowan scorched him with a dark look. "Just for the record, that's never going to happen."

"I was kidding. Well, mostly."

Rowan shook her head. "No dirty pictures."

"Yeah, yeah." Quinn rubbed the sleep out of his eyes as he focused on the camera. "What are you doing?"

"Looking for photos of Selena."

"Oh." Quinn straightened as he watched Rowan flip through the photos. "If the omen is gone, that means she's in the clear, right?"

"In theory. I mean, I guess an accident could happen, but generally once the omen is gone, so is the threat."

"What do we have?"

Rowan clicked on the first photo of Selena she found and peered closer. "No omen. It's gone."

"Are you sure?" Quinn leaned closer.

"This is the first photo I took yesterday," Rowan offered. "The omen was right here." She pointed for emphasis. "Now it's gone."

"So ... that's a good thing, right?"

Rowan nodded. "According to this she's no longer in danger."

"Yeah, I still want to know why she was in danger in the first place."

"That makes two of us."

Quinn smiled as he kissed her neck. "That's why we're such a good pair."

"Is this you being romantic?"

"Maybe."

"Well, let's see what you've got. I'm starving but mildly curious."

"Way to keep the pressure off."

"I do my best."

10

TEN

Quinn and Rowan had breakfast in the main dining room. Despite the events of the previous day, the meal was a relaxed affair, both happy they were back in sync with nothing standing between them.

They were drinking coffee and making plans for the day when Anthony approached.

"I don't want to disturb you."

Quinn shifted in his chair. "Oh, well ... ."

"You're not disturbing us." Rowan offered up a friendly smile. "We were just finishing up. Did you find anything after we went to bed last night?"

"Just a celebration of sorts at the tiki bar." Anthony took one of the open chairs. "I was wondering if you found anything."

"Not yet, but I'm going to stop and see Selena as soon as I'm done here," Quinn said. "She's going to be released from the medical wing before noon and I want to get her statement on the record before that happens. She was too worked up last night to give us one."

"Do you mind if I go with you?"

Quinn shook his head. "Not at all. I understand this is a concern for you as much as me."

"I'm more confused than anything else," Anthony said. "I've been trying to come up with a motive and I can't."

Quinn sipped his coffee. "What do you know about Selena?"

"Just what Andrea told me."

"Which is?"

"She's a competent diver. She has a bit of a wild streak, but that's not uncommon given her line of work. It's something of a daredevil field. Selena has been known to purposely hop in shark cages with cameras and she's licensed for dangerous dives. That attracts a certain ... um ... personality type."

Rowan was confused. "I don't know what that means."

"It means that she's known to take chances with her personal and professional life," Quinn supplied. "People like Selena like living on the edge. That means they're more likely to skirt the edge of reason, perhaps do things normal people would find uncomfortable."

"That doesn't explain why she would be attacked, though," Rowan pointed out. "I'm more worried about the motivations of the person who tried to throw her over the edge than why Selena likes to be wild and crazy."

"That's a fair point, but Selena must have done something to draw attention to herself," Anthony argued. "People don't get attacked for no reason when they're minding their own business."

"I was on the deck with Selena for the bulk of the afternoon yesterday," Rowan offered. "She didn't do anything but hang out with her friends."

"Yes, but we don't know what she did before that."

Quinn ran his thumb over his bottom lip as he considered the situation. "Whoever it was managed to steal a key card from one of the maids. He had to have it planned ahead of time. I talked to the maid in question last night and she swears she didn't see anyone out of the ordinary watching her.

"She was in the gym for a bit and then she went and got her hair done," he continued. "She was with friends and no one saw anyone following. Still, someone managed to steal her key card without anyone seeing, and she's fairly positive it had to be in the break room because that's where she was when she noticed it was missing. That, to me, seems to indicate we're dealing with a professional."

Rowan was horrified. "A professional killer?"

Quinn shrugged. "Maybe not that far. Someone who knew what he was doing, though. Someone who could fly under the radar."

"You're insinuating it was someone on my security staff," Anthony said, stiffening. "That's what you're saying, right?"

"Not necessarily." Quinn remained calm, sensing there was a chance Anthony might fly off the handle. "I will say that the bulk of my security team is made up of former military personnel and retired police officers. They know what they're doing in a tense situation, but they're not the sort of professional who could steal a key card without anyone noticing."

"What about new personnel?" Anthony challenged. "Maybe someone slipped on the ship without you knowing. You can't go over every personnel file. That would be ... a lot of freaking work."

"It was a lot of work when I first joined the crew," Quinn clarified. "It's not all that much work now. We do see a decent amount of turnover, but it honestly never jumps by more than five or six bodies with each trip. I go over each file before okaying a hire."

"And you have that much power?" Anthony was impressed. "I thought you were just a figurehead."

Quinn could have taken the statement as an insult ... but he didn't. "One of the reasons I signed on for this gig was the freedom they allowed me in my contract. I wanted the power to veto people if I found something in their background checks that worried me. Surprisingly, I've been given a bit of omnipotence since I arrived and it's worked out well."

"Until now," Anthony pointed out. "We have no idea if the attacker was one of your people or one of mine."

"No, but I intend to find out." Quinn took another sip of coffee before turning his full attention to Rowan. He wanted to discuss a few things with her, but couldn't given Anthony's apparent interest in staying close. "What are you going to do today?"

Rowan recognized his tone and adjusted hers accordingly. "I'm going to hang out on deck and take photos of everyone before the big arrival. That happens before dinner, so I figured that would take up the bulk of my afternoon. I also plan on stopping in to see Selena, but I'll wait until you guys are done questioning her."

"That sounds like a plan." Quinn patted the top of Rowan's hand. "I'll take you to a nice dinner tonight once we hit the island. I've been here once before and I know a nice place. They have seafood pasta that you'll absolutely go gaga over."

Rowan snorted. "You just like it when I go gaga."

"You have no idea." Quinn flicked his eyes to Anthony and found the security guru watching the exchange with curious eyes. "As for us, I want to look at the hoodie found in the trash receptacle last night. I'm going to guess there are no identifying markers on it, but I want to make sure. Then I figured we would hit Selena and go from there."

"I think those are our best options," Anthony agreed. "I know this sounds selfish, but I'm hoping the culprit turns out to be a member of your crew rather than mine. If he's part of my crew ... well ... it won't be good."

"Why not?" Rowan asked.

"Because that means they've got a live wire in their midst," Quinn supplied. "That's the last thing he needs considering all the attention that's going to be foisted on this dive. All eyes are going to be on them and he doesn't need news getting out that he's got a rogue working for him."

"Which is exactly why I want to figure this out before we dock if I can." Anthony pushed himself to a standing position. "Are you ready?"

Quinn bobbed his head. "Just give me a minute with Rowan. I'll meet you by the door."

"Oh, are you going to get all lovey-dovey?" Anthony's tone was derisive, but his eyes were lit with interest.

"Probably." Quinn saw no reason to be embarrassed. "I won't be but a minute."

Anthony nodded to Rowan before moving away from the table. Quinn made sure he was out of earshot before speaking again.

"You're going to take photos of everyone you can find, aren't you?"

"Do you have a better idea?" Rowan asked. "Just because Selena no longer has the omen hanging over her, that doesn't mean others don't. I figure it's worth a try ... especially since I don't have much else to do this afternoon."

"I think it's worth a try, too. I want you to be careful, though. No wandering around to the front or back of the boat by yourself. You stick close to large crowds when you're taking photos."

Rowan balked. "You think I'm a target?"

"I think I don't want you becoming a target so you'd better stay safe." Quinn smacked a loud kiss against the corner of her mouth. "Be good. Be safe. Keep in touch."

"Sir, yes, sir." Rowan mock saluted, causing Quinn to grin.

"I'll take you to a romantic dinner tonight to make up for last night ... and, er, the night before."

Rowan's expression softened. "That sounds like a plan."

"Good." This time the kiss they shared was softer and full of promise. "I'll be in touch. Stay safe."

ANTHONY FOLLOWED QUINN through the labyrinth of hallways that led to the medical ward. Even though the silence that descended over the men was friendly, Quinn wasn't an idiot and knew the security guru was barely refraining from asking questions.

"You might as well get out what you want to get out," Quinn suggested, slowing his pace. "It's going to be a long day if you spend the entire afternoon biting your tongue."

Anthony's expression was sheepish. "I'm sorry. I'm just ... it's just ... well ... your relationship with Rowan intrigues me."

That wasn't the response Quinn was expecting. "And why is that?"

"I would think a man in your position wouldn't want to be tied down," Anthony noted. "You're on a ship surrounded by women in bikinis all day. You could have a different woman in every port."

"I could," Quinn agreed. "That's not what I want, though."

"And what do you want?"

"Before Rowan arrived on the ship, I wanted to be left alone. I was something of a loner, although I had friends, and I was more interested in brooding and reading than anything else."

"You sound like a geek."

Quinn snorted. "Believe it or not, you're not the first person to tell me that this week."

"So she changed things for you?"

"She did." Quinn scratched at his cheek as he held open the door that led to the medical bay. "She's interesting ... and funny ... and she has a smile that lights up a room. That changed things for me."

"And you really don't want to have a woman in every port?" Anthony challenged. "I mean, to me, that would be the biggest benefit of this job."

"And to me that sounds like the worst way to spend my time ever. I honestly don't want a girl in every port. I'm fine with my one girl."

"She's great," Anthony offered. "Don't get me wrong, I find her intriguing. If she wasn't very obviously gone for you, I would totally try to make her my girl for this port."

Quinn scowled. "Don't say things like that. You're going to force me to pick a fight with you and I'm sure I'll lose."

Anthony chuckled. "That might work out to your benefit. If I beat you up, she'll dress up like a nurse to take care of you."

"I'll file that away for later." Quinn strode into the medical bay and fixed the doctor, Jordan Cooper, with a pointed look. "How is our patient?"

Jordan, who started out as a plastic surgeon in Los Angeles before deciding he was destined to be a cruise liner healer, was relaxed and happy as he sipped a green tea concoction. "She's perfectly fine. I honestly don't think she needed to spend the night here."

"She was an emotional wreck last night," Quinn countered. "I thought it was best if you drugged her so she could sleep."

"I gave her a mild tranquilizer. She made it through the night without any nightmares, at least as far as the reports I got. Your men didn't allow anyone in or out, so she was the only one here."

"Is she up now?"

"She is, and she's making noise about wanting to leave," Jordan replied. "I figured you would want to talk to her first so I put her off."

"You figured right." Quinn offered up a nod in thanks before moving past Jordan and walking into Selena's room. She sat on her bed, a blank expression on her face, and the look she shot Quinn when she realized she wasn't alone was nothing short of adoring.

"It's you."

"It's me." Quinn felt mildly uncomfortable when Selena grabbed his hand and pressed it to the spot between her breasts. "Um ... how are you feeling?"

Anthony's eyes flashed with amusement as he moved to the other side of the bed. "Do you remember what happened last night?"

Selena furrowed her brow when Quinn managed to extricate his hand, giving him a pointed look before turning her full attention to Anthony. "I remember everything that happened last night. I was almost killed ... and this man saved me." Her voice was almost a soft coo.

Even though it was a serious situation, it took everything Quinn had not to burst out laughing at Selena's overacting. "Yes, well, that's my job."

"It's both our jobs," Anthony corrected. "That's why we're here, Selena. We need to know what happened yesterday."

"I don't know what to tell you." Selena was much more in control than she had been the previous evening. "I spent the afternoon hanging out with people from my team. We had a few drinks, although nothing major. Mostly piña coladas and margaritas.

"We were going to head in and get changed for dinner when I remembered I forgot my flip flops by my chair so I headed back. I wasn't even back to the chair when that guy approached me."

"Did you see his face?" Quinn asked. "I know he was wearing a hoodie, but you must have seen something."

"Nothing more than a flash of eyes."

"What color eyes?"

"Brown."

"Could you tell his skin color?" Anthony asked. "I know you saw very little, but what about his skin color?"

"And eyebrow color," Quinn added. "Did you see a hint of facial hair?"

"Geez, you guys ask a lot of questions," Selena complained. "As for answers, I didn't see any facial hair. He had darker eyebrows ... at least I think. He was white. That's all I know. It happened really fast and I was so intent on fighting him off I didn't even think to look at his face.

"Then, when he threw me over the edge, all I could think was that I was going to die," she continued, her expression angelic when she turned back to Quinn. "Then you showed up and saved me. It was ... glorious."

Quinn touched the tip of his tongue to his top lip, dumbfounded. "Oh, well ... um ... hmm."

Anthony was beyond entertained, although he interjected himself into the conversation to save Quinn from further embarrassment. "I believe Mr. Davenport is uncomfortable being heralded as a hero."

"He *is* a hero, though," Selena stressed. "He's my hero."

"I didn't do it alone," Quinn reminded her. "I had help."

"You did?" Selena knit her eyebrows. "Who?"

"My girlfriend." Quinn hated dropping the "girlfriend" card, but it was obvious it was necessary to nip Selena's mild infatuation in the bud. "She held on to me so I could have the leverage to grab you. Without her, neither one of us would be here."

"I don't remember anyone else being there," Selena mused. "How odd."

"Yeah, totally." Quinn rolled his eyes until they landed on Anthony. "I think our next step should be going over the video footage again – and there are gaps that our guy managed to exploit, so it won't be easy. I don't know what else to do."

"You could walk me back to my room," Selena suggested hopefully.

"My men will do that." Quinn kept his smile in place even though his skin was crawling. "I have two security officers waiting for you on the other side of the door. They would be happy to walk you to your room."

Selena made a face. "They're not you."

"They're not, no," Quinn agreed. "I have other things to focus on, though. I'm afraid that's the best I can do."

"Whatever." Selena's irritation was evident as she crossed her arms over her chest. "This is turning into a sucky morning."

"Take heart," Anthony prodded. "We'll be at our destination by nightfall. By this time tomorrow, we'll be wet and looking for treasure. That's got to make you feel better, right?"

Selena brightened considerably. "Absolutely."

"That's what I thought."

11

ELEVEN

Rowan snapped photos of everyone she could find. She made sure to stay out in the open – more for Quinn's sake than her own – and she sat down in the shade next to the tiki bar shortly before lunch to load the images on to her computer so she could study them up close.

She couldn't find the omen in any photos.

That was a good thing. At least that's what she kept telling herself. Still, she couldn't shake the feeling that she was missing something.

That's where Selena found her an hour into her photo search.

"Um ... are you busy?"

"Oh, hey." Rowan moved to shut her computer, as if she had something on the screen she shouldn't, but ultimately thought better of it. "How are you feeling?"

"Much better, thank you." Selena took the open seat across from Rowan and offered up a wan smile. "Your boyfriend came to see me a few hours ago."

"Yeah. He said he was going to. Did you give him any information that can help us catch this guy?"

Selena shook her head. "I can't remember a lot of it. I know that sounds weird, but my memory is all jumbled up. I didn't even remember you were there until he told me."

Rowan didn't know what to make of that information. "Oh ... um ...."

"It's not a dig at you," Selena offered. "Quinn said he wouldn't have been able to save me if you didn't help. I'm grateful."

"I'm not sure how true that is. He provided all the muscle. I basically sat on his feet to make sure he didn't accidentally fall over."

Selena snickered, genuinely amused. "He says it was more than that."

"Well, he's sweet on me so he says things like that even when they're not true."

Selena's smile flickered, but just barely. "Yes, well, I believe I should be thankful for your help. I also believe I should probably apologize."

Rowan's eyebrows flew up her forehead. "Apologize?"

"I kind of hit on your boyfriend ... several times ... when he came to interview me. I was just so thankful and he's kind of hot. He had to put me in my place a little bit. I didn't even realize what I was doing until I stepped back and thought about it."

Even though she knew she should probably be offended, Rowan was amused. "That's okay. It was a trying situation for you. I think it's called transference when a life-changing ordeal makes you attracted to the person you deem your hero after a traumatic event."

Selena chuckled, the sound low and throaty. "Oh, I would've been attracted to him no matter what. He's extremely handsome. I simply think I took it a step too far. He looked ... uncomfortable."

"He'll survive. You wouldn't believe how many people hit on him during a normal cruise. He's extremely popular."

Selena relaxed a bit as she leaned back in her chair. "Well, thank you anyway. So ... what are you doing?"

"Trying to pretend my boss isn't paying me for nothing on this particular trip. Generally I'm busy from breakfast to dinner taking photos, but since you guys aren't here on a vacation ... it's been something of an odd fit for me."

"I can see that. Still, it's exciting. Do you dive?"

Rowan shook her head. "I grew up in Michigan. We don't dive there."

"Actually, that's not true. A lot of people dive in the Great Lakes. Still, I get what you're saying. Hopefully you'll get to see the site, though."

"You must be excited," Rowan noted. "You get to go down with the first group, right?"

Selena bobbed her head. "It's exciting. It's a little daunting. I've been on discovery dives before, but this one is being touted as a huge deal. I've been looking at maps and everything, which I generally don't do. I found a unique one for that particular part of the ocean on eBay of all places, if you can believe that."

Rowan cocked an eyebrow. "On eBay?"

Selena shrugged. "Hey, you take these things where you can find them. This is supposed to be a tricky spot and I don't want to be the one to screw things up."

"Plus the water is supposed to be dangerous. Does that worry you?"

"Nah. I know what I'm doing in the water. We dive with partners and keep an eye on each other. It's when I'm out of the water that I tend to make my mistakes. I rarely make them when I'm in the water."

"Still, I can't wait to see what you guys find," Rowan enthused. "I'm betting it's going to be some unique stuff."

"I'm a little excited, too. It would be more fun if we got to keep what we find, but this could be a historic discovery so we had to sign explicit contracts saying we wouldn't pocket any of the goods."

"Still, you'll get to see them. That would be enough for me."

"I would prefer the money but seeing the wreck will still be exhilarating."

"Quinn loves history," Rowan supplied. "He's been reading up on The Conqueror. I hope he has a chance to at least go out there and see the ship, although I'm not sure what he'll be able to see from the surface."

"We're going to have submersibles, too," Selena offered. "I'm sure he'll be able to get on one of those."

"That sounds like fun. I hope that works out for him."

The two women chatted for a bit longer, Selena making nice and promising to refrain from flirting with Quinn before departing. Rowan took the opportunity to return to her photographs, although her heart wasn't in the search. She was positive the omen wasn't there. That should have made her happy. Instead it made her uneasy.

"You look lost in thought."

Rowan jerked her head to the left at the sound of the voice, working overtime to hide her distaste when Nick floated into view. "I was merely debating what to do with these photographs. No one seems excited about them ... and I doubt I'll sell many. I figure I should probably still load them to the online portal to be on the safe side."

"It couldn't hurt." Nick was all smiles when he sat across from her. He had an unerring ability to make Rowan feel as if she was the only person in the room – er, more like the world – when he focused on her. "And how are you today?"

"What do you mean by that?" Rowan didn't intend to come off as suspicious, but the words were out of her mouth before she could think better about uttering them.

"I mean that you had a very eventful night." Nick's expression was bland, although his eyes gleamed when they locked with Rowan's. "You saved a life, if I'm not mistaken."

"Oh, *that*." Rowan let loose with a cross between a sigh and a giggle. "I didn't save a life. I held on to a pair of legs. Quinn saved a life."

"That's not how I heard it. I heard you ran toward danger and helped save one of our divers from certain death."

"Certain death?" Rowan tilted her head to the side. "That's a little ... dramatic."

"So, you're saying if you and Mr. Davenport hadn't been there, Selena would have been perfectly fine?"

"Well, no," Rowan hedged. "She definitely needed help."

"So you are, indeed, a hero."

"Yeah, this conversation is making me uncomfortable." Rowan shifted on her chair. "What about you? You must be upset to know one of your employees was almost killed. That can't be something you want to hear."

"Certainly not," Nick agreed. "I've had a long talk with Anthony and he assures me that he believes our team is safe and secure. That's the most important thing."

"I don't know how he can say that," Rowan argued. "Selena almost died last night. That's pretty far from safe."

"Yes, but the individual who attacked her was from your crew, not ours."

Rowan wrinkled her nose. "No, the attacker stole a key card from one of our crew members," she corrected. "We have no idea if the attacker was one of your people or ours. Given the nature of the attack, though, it doesn't make much sense for it to be someone from our side of the aisle."

Nick steepled his fingers as he rested his elbows on the table and leaned back in his chair. "What do you mean by that?"

"It wasn't a sexual attack," Rowan explained. "It was something else."

"But Anthony said he believed it was a sexual attack. Why would he lie?"

Rowan was uncomfortable with the question. "Maybe he didn't lie. Maybe he thought he was telling the truth. He said the same thing last night, although Quinn didn't happen to agree with him.

"The thing is, whoever attacked Selena tried to throw her over the side of the ship," she continued. "That doesn't seem like a good way to get sexual gratification to me."

"I hadn't even considered that." Nick looked lost in thought.

"Why do you think the attack occurred?"

Rowan shrugged. "I honestly have no idea. I don't think it was a sexual attack, though. I think it was something else. What is anyone's guess."

"You make a very good point." Nick's smile brightened as he returned to the here and now. "You're a very interesting woman. I read your file – and went back over it again after our previous conversation – and it seems you were left to your own devices at a young age. How did that work out for you?"

The question threw Rowan for a loop. "I'm not sure what you mean by that."

"Your mother died when you were barely into your teens and then your father disappeared when you were eighteen. You were essentially abandoned. That couldn't have been easy for you."

Rowan's agitation threatened to overwhelm her. "I don't really think that's any of your concern."

"I'm merely curious."

"And yet it's none of your business."

"What's none of his business?" Quinn appeared at the edge of the table, widening his eyes when neither Nick nor Rowan opted to look in his direction. He sensed a great deal of animosity emanating from Rowan, enough that he thought better about resting a hand on her shoulder. "Is something going on?"

Nick broke eye contact first, offering Quinn a friendly smile as he got to his feet. "We were talking about your life-saving efforts last night. Well done." He clapped Quinn on the shoulder. "I'm glad we're going to get to spend time together. I love being in the presence of heroes."

Quinn balked. "I'm not sure I would phrase it quite like that."

"You didn't. I did." Nick's smile was so wide it almost engulfed his entire face. The sentiment didn't make it all the way to his eyes, though. "I should get going. We're due to dock in about two hours. I'm looking forward to it, but I have a lot of things to ready before then."

"Yeah, well ... ." Quinn wasn't sure what to say so he let it go. He waited until Nick was out of earshot to turn his full attention on Rowan. "Do you want to tell me what that was about?"

Rowan pursed her lips. "He makes me uncomfortable."

Quinn took the seat Nick abandoned moments before and snagged her hand. "How? Is he saying things to you?"

"Not like you mean," Rowan replied. "He hasn't been sexually aggressive or anything. He has been ... weird."

"I'm going to need more information than that."

"I don't have more information than that," Rowan said. "Ever since that first moment I saw him at the restaurant, I've felt like I should know him. I can't put my finger on it. It's starting to mess with my mind, though."

Quinn licked his lips, his mind busy. "Well, if it's one thing I know it's that you're intuitive and smart. You read people well. If you think you should know him, then maybe you do know him."

"Don't you think I would remember if we'd met before?" Rowan challenged. "We've spent enough time together now that I should be able to place his face."

"I don't know." Quinn wasn't sure how to appease her. "Maybe ... ." He broke off, tilting his head to the side. "You know what? Give me your computer."

Rowan pushed her laptop across the table without complaint, watching as Quinn minimized the portal window and brought up a search window she'd never seen before. "What's that?"

"It's what I use to run background checks on those applying for jobs. It's not in-depth, but it does give me the basics. It also flags certain things that might require further investigation."

"Like what?"

Quinn remained focused on the computer screen as he typed. "Like court files. I can't read the court files with this program, but I will be alerted to their presence."

"Oh, so you know where to look."

"Exactly."

"And what are you looking for now?"

"Whatever I can find on Nicholas Green."

Rowan was intrigued so she grabbed her chair and slid closer to Quinn so she could watch him work. "Do you think you'll find anything?"

Quinn's grin was crooked as he slid a sidelong look in her direction. "Under normal circumstances it would drive me nuts to have someone watching me this way."

"Sorry." Rowan made to move, but he stopped her with a shake of his head.

"I kind of like it with you," Quinn supplied. "That might make me sick ... or a bit strange ... but I can't help it."

Rowan snickered. "I think you're trying to schmooze me before our romantic dinner tonight."

"Schmooze?"

"You heard me. Here's a tip, though, pal ... I think you're going to get lucky regardless."

Quinn barked out a laugh, genuinely amused. "You are my favorite person in the world these days. Do you know that?"

Rowan's cheeks flushed with pleasure. "Thank you." She lowered her gaze. "I feel the same way."

"I especially like how flustered you get when I say things like that." Quinn leaned over and kissed the corner of her mouth before turning his attention back to the computer screen. "Let's see what we've got, shall we?"

Rowan flicked her eyes to the information scrolling across the screen. Much of it made very little sense to her, but Quinn seemed to grasp it. "Anything?"

"Well, yes and no." Quinn scratched at the back of his head. "Nicholas Green has only been with Outer Boundaries for a few months."

"That shouldn't be surprising. Anthony told us that, right? I swear he said that."

"I think he did, but I didn't pay much attention." Quinn's expression was hard to read. "Before that he worked for a travel company in Australia."

"Australia? That's quite the change in locales."

"Yeah."

"What about before that?"

Quinn shifted his eyes to Rowan, something dark flitting through them. "Well, that's what's really interesting. It seems that Nicholas Green hasn't always existed."

Rowan stilled, confused. "I don't know what that means."

"It means that he's only been around – at least operating under this name – for the past ten years."

"Where was he before that?"

"I don't know. The 'who' and the 'where' both seem intriguing to me."

"But ... I don't know what to say. It seems important and yet I'm not sure how."

"It's definitely important." Quinn moved his hand from the laptop keyboard and rested it on Rowan's thigh, giving her a reassuring squeeze as he scanned the deck for signs of Nick. He was gone, though. "We need more information."

"How are you going to get that?"

Quinn smirked. "I have my ways. Don't worry about that."

"Your friend on the mainland?"

Quinn's smile slipped. "Do you have to ruin all my fun? Men like to be mysterious, Ro. You're squelching my vibe."

Even though it was a serious situation, Rowan could do nothing but laugh. "That is the funniest thing you've ever said."

Quinn was happy to have lightened the mood. "Good, but that doesn't change the fact that this is weird. I'm going to have to do a more in-depth search."

"What do you think you'll find when you do?"

"I have no idea, but the possibilities don't exactly make me happy."

12

TWELVE

Quinn got in touch with his associate, gave him a brief rundown of what they were dealing with, and then wheedled and cajoled until Fred Delmore gave in and agreed to help.

"I do more work for you than myself," Fred complained as Quinn watched Rowan change into her new dress so they could disembark for dinner. "You're a lot of work for a dude who is supposed to be in charge."

Quinn rolled his eyes. "It's one search, Fred. There's no reason to whine."

"I'm not whining."

"See, from where I'm sitting, it sounds a lot like whining."

"Then perhaps you should move your chair."

"I'm liking my view a lot right now," Quinn said as Rowan leaned over to fasten the buckles on her shoes. "It's very ... pretty."

Rowan realized Quinn was talking about her and sent him a wicked smile over her shoulder. Fred, who could see nothing, read his friend's voice perfectly.

"You're not alone, are you?"

"What?" Quinn forced himself back to the here and now. "What does that have to do with anything?"

"You're with your pretty girlfriend," Fred teased. "I liked the photos you sent to me, by the way. She's quite the looker."

"She is quite the looker," Quinn agreed, smirking when Rowan's cheeks flushed with color. "She also knows we're talking about her and she's all kinds of embarrassed."

"I prefer women who don't get embarrassed," Fred noted. "They're more willing to do lewd and outrageous acts if they don't have the embarrassment gene."

"And on that note...." Quinn made a clucking sound with his tongue.

"Yeah, yeah." Fred turned serious. "I'll run the name, but odds are I won't have any results for you until tomorrow at the earliest."

"I figured that would be the case. It's fine. We're going out to dinner tonight anyway. Then, tomorrow, we're going to see the location of the ship find for the first time. I'll have a lot on my plate."

"Does that mean you don't want me to put a rush on the search?"

"No, I definitely want you to put a rush on it," Quinn countered. "I can't shake the feeling that something odd is going on here."

"And it doesn't help that this Nicholas Green fellow is interested in your woman."

"No, it doesn't." Quinn smiled at Rowan as she grabbed her purse from the bedside table. She was ready, which meant it was finally time to spend some quality time together. "See what you can get me. If it's something big, send a text on my phone. I'll have it with me."

"I'll do my best, but like I said, I don't expect to start getting the early stuff until tomorrow. The stuff from the deep run will probably take even longer than that."

"Do your best."

IT WAS **A QUIET BUT** beautiful night when Quinn and Rowan hit El Demonio. Rowan made the occasional visit to port stops during normal trips, but Quinn only bothered when she was with him. On the flip side, they liked a little variation for their meal offerings, and tonight was no exception.

"I'm thinking Italian with a seafood flair." Quinn linked his fingers with Rowan's as he led her down the street. The sun was dipping in the sky and it would be dark long before they made it back to the ship. Still, it was a relatively safe area and he wasn't overly worried. That didn't mean he wouldn't watch their surroundings as they cut through the heavily-populated tourist hub.

"That sounds good to me," Rowan said. "We should probably avoid too much garlic if we want to enjoy the whole night, though."

The double meaning of her words wasn't lost on Quinn. "Or we could both eat garlic."

"Stink together?"

"I just really like garlic. I don't think it stinks."

"Okay, we can both eat garlic." Rowan was in a good mood and she stopped at a small jewelry display, a pair of earrings catching her eye. "We don't get to do this often, do we?"

"What? Talk in sexy code?"

Rowan giggled, the sound shooting through Quinn and warming his heart. "We happen to do that quite often."

"Not often enough." Quinn watched her hold the earrings up to the side of her face, enjoying the way she smiled at herself in the mirror. He snagged the earrings from her before she could return them to the display and handed them to the man watching from the end of the kiosk. "We'll take these."

The man beamed. "Very good choice." He grabbed them and looked to the back so he could find the price, but Quinn had the money out to pay before he could request the cash.

"You don't have to do that," Rowan supplied. "I could buy them for myself."

"Maybe I want to buy them for you. Did you consider that?"

"No. I thought you were buying dinner."

"I can buy more than one thing." Quinn claimed his change and handed the small bag with the earrings to Rowan. "Something to remember our night."

Rowan accepted the bag with a grin. "I think we would've remembered it no matter what."

"Because of all the sexy talk?"

Rowan snorted. "Because we're together."

"Ah, that's far more sweet than what I was thinking."

They resumed their walk, Quinn swinging their hands in beat with their footsteps. It wasn't until they closed in on the restaurant that he spoke again.

"I don't want you being afraid or upset."

The conversational shift took Rowan by surprise. "I'm not. I'm having a good time."

"I know that. I mean about Nicholas Green. We'll figure out what's going on. It could still be something simple."

"You don't believe that, though."

"I don't know what I believe. I can't say that I trust him – he's been far too interested in you from the start – but I'm not getting a creepy sexual vibe from him so I don't know what to think."

Rowan arched an eyebrow. "Would you prefer a creepy sexual vibe?"

Quinn shrugged. "It would give me something to go on. If I thought he was merely attracted to you, I could have a talk with him and make sure he understands to stay away from you."

"He hasn't done anything overt," Rowan argued. "He hasn't touched me ... or suggested he be able to touch me ... or even looked at me in a way that indicates he wants to touch me."

"There's a lot of talk about touching here," Quinn noted. "How about we keep the touching talk between us? I definitely want to touch you later, but I'm hungry. You're threatening to ruin my appetite."

"Ha, ha." Rowan poked his muscled stomach. "He makes me uneasy, but it's not in the same way that other people make me uneasy."

Quinn cast her a sidelong look. "Who else makes you uneasy?"

"On this particular trip, no one. I've had my fair share of run-ins with pervs, though. There's something about a single woman carrying a camera that makes gross men say the darndest things."

"Yeah, that makes me want to lock you in your cabin for the rest of our lives."

"That might be fun. We should plan a weekend around something like that."

"I'm open to that plan when we can make it work." Quinn squeezed her hand as he directed her toward a restaurant he'd heard good things about. "This is the place."

Rowan beamed. "Bring on the garlic."

Quinn matched her smile for smile until he stepped into the restaurant and ran smack-dab into Anthony and Andrea. They sat at a table in the center of the small bistro, their heads bent together in conversation until they noticed Quinn and Rowan by the front door. The duo flashed bright smiles upon realizing their dinner party would be expanding.

"Join us," Andrea insisted, patting the chair to her left. "We were just talking about you."

Quinn tried to keep his smile in place ... and failed miserably. "What are the odds?"

Rowan tossed him a sympathetic smile. "It's going to be okay. We'll still have time to ourselves."

Quinn wasn't convinced. "Do you think they'll take it the wrong way if we turn and run?"

"Probably."

Quinn heaved out a sigh, resigned. "Fine. I'm not going to forget this, though. I'm going to find a way to make them pay."

"I'm going to help you."

"SO, **WHAT DO YOU** two have planned tonight?"

Andrea was amiable and chatty as she broke a breadstick in half and dipped it in olive oil.

"It definitely wasn't this," Quinn grumbled. He'd been less than enthusiastic since sitting, forcing Anthony to get up and move closer to Andrea so he could have the spot next to Rowan. His dour mood wasn't lost on his dinner companions.

"You don't have to sit with us," Anthony offered. "We invited you because it was the polite thing to do. If you want to go someplace else ... ."

"Ignore him," Rowan offered, patting Quinn's knee under the table. "We're both tired after last night. He gets crabby when he's tired."

Quinn shot her a dark look. "I'm not crabby."

"You definitely seem crabby," Andrea countered.

"Yes, well ... it's been a long day." Quinn leaned back in his chair and rolled his neck until it cracked. "I don't mean to be rude."

Anthony snickered. "You don't care how rude you are. You're just mad we interrupted whatever romantic date you had planned."

Quinn didn't bother denying it. "So what?"

"Oh, why can't I find a man like you?" Andrea complained. "You're actually upset about missing a romantic date. The last guy I was with thought a romantic date included ordering pizza and watching porn."

"That's how all my dates go," Anthony teased.

Andrea was blasé. "Figures."

Rowan pursed her lips to keep from laughing. "That sounds kind of like the last guy I dated before I lost my job and came to work on The Bounding Storm."

"Tell me about him," Andrea prodded.

"No, I don't want to hear about him," Quinn countered. "Let's not talk about old boyfriends and girlfriends. Let's focus on current things."

Anthony tapped his fingers on the table. "Not all of us have current things to talk about."

Quinn straightened in his chair. "What do you mean? I thought you two were ... you know."

"No, we just met each other," Anthony countered. "We get along fine, which is good because we have to share responsibility on this job, but we're not into each other like that."

"You're not?" Rowan knit her eyebrows as she glanced between them. "How come? You're both hot and in great shape. You look good together. Why not give it a chance?"

"Because unlike you, we don't have a home base," Anthony answered. "In theory, it sounds great for us to have a nice roll in the hay ... er, waves ... and then go on our merry way. Do you know why that doesn't work?"

"I'm fascinated to hear why," Quinn drawled as he grabbed a breadstick and shoved it in his mouth.

"I can already tell that Captain Killjoy is going to be a great dinner companion," Andrea drawled. "If I had the ability to be offended, I would totally be upset that he doesn't want to eat with me."

"It's not that," Quinn protested. "I don't really care about eating with you. I wanted to eat with her ... alone." He jerked a thumb in Rowan's direction. "We've had zero chance to be alone in days."

"Didn't you leave together last night?" Anthony challenged.

"Yes, but we were both exhausted after a long day. I was still recovering from my hangover ... which was your fault, by the way."

"Yes, I shoved the beer bottle into your mouth and forced you to drink it." Anthony rolled his eyes. "You need to chill. You'll have plenty of time to be alone after dinner. I'm actually glad we ran into you because there are a few things I want to discuss."

"Such as?"

"Well, for starters, we're taking the initial team over first thing in the morning." Anthony was all business as he shifted the conversation to something more important than Quinn's whiny attitude. "We can't dive until after ten, but we hope to have things scoped out before then. The submersible should be wet by the time we hit the water."

Quinn perked up. "Submersible?"

"Oh, yeah, I heard some mention of that," Rowan said. "I thought you might want to go down in the submersible to see the ship if they allow it."

"Submersible?" Anthony wrinkled his forehead. "I thought you were diving with us as soon as we cleared the route."

"Diving?" Rowan turned to Quinn, confused. "You know how to dive?"

"Know how to dive?" Anthony laughed so loud it caused Rowan to jolt. "He's certified for every sort of dive there is. It's not as if he's a beginner."

"Oh." Rowan felt stupid for not knowing that. "Of course you are. You were in the military for years. I guess I didn't realize that meant you could dive."

"The type of diving I did during my tours was different," Quinn offered. "It wasn't recreational diving. I started doing the other during my off time. I keep up on my certification. This job has actually been good for that because I get a decent amount of down time."

"So ... you're diving with them?" Rowan didn't know what to make of the news. "I thought it was dangerous."

"Quinn is a tough guy," Anthony said. "He'll be perfectly fine."

Rowan wasn't convinced and yet she instinctively understood she shouldn't make a big deal about Quinn's potential dive, especially in front of an audience. Anthony wasn't the type of man to understand her worry. "Well ... I guess you'll get to see the wreck up close and personal. That's what you wanted."

"Don't sound so excited," Andrea deadpanned. "You're acting as if he's about to dive to his death rather than actually be able to touch history. This is an important dive."

Rowan was getting tired of hearing those exact words. "I'm well aware that it's an important dive. I didn't say anything to the contrary."

"And yet you're upset," Andrea noted. "How come?"

"I'm not upset." Rowan forced a tight smile. "I'm just ... surprised. I didn't know Quinn was going to be diving. I feel like a fool for thinking that he would want to go down in the submersible."

"I want to do that, too," Quinn said. "I haven't made up my mind on the diving yet."

"You haven't?"

"Yeah, you haven't?" Anthony offered up an exaggerated face. "The other night you were all for it."

"I was also drunk the other night and thought dyeing my hair pink sounded like a good idea."

Anthony snickered. "I kind of forgot about that."

"I didn't." Quinn rolled his neck. "As for the diving, I want to see the initial reports before making a decision. Even if I wanted to do it tomorrow, though, I wouldn't have the time. I have to make sure the salon is ready for artifacts and watch the area between the ship and site for transportation issues first."

"I've got all that covered," Anthony pointed out.

"And yet I still have to check on it myself." Quinn's tone was firm. "Tomorrow is going to be a busy day. I'm not ruling out a dive the following day ... or even later in the week. I have other things I need to focus on tomorrow, though."

"Okay, but you're going to be missing out."

Rowan had no trouble reading the looks Anthony and Andrea shared. They thought Quinn was being an idiot to give up on such a unique opportunity. As worried as she was for his safety, Rowan couldn't help but wonder if it was her fear holding him back.

She knew Quinn had a life before her. She knew he was good at whatever he did while in the military, although he was careful to keep those details from her. She figured that was because he didn't want to talk about the lives he'd seen lost, and possibly even the lives he'd taken. She understood that and didn't push.

What she hadn't taken into account was the fact that not everything Quinn dealt with, not all the ways he spent his time while serving overseas, were dark and terrible. There was a lot of fun in there, good memories, and even rowdy times.

She didn't want to take an important opportunity away from him and she couldn't shake the idea that he was turning down the chance to dive early simply because of her. Their fight had left him shaken and remorseful. Even though he screwed up, she didn't want him to dwell on it. It was hardly life-shattering stuff.

"I still think you should dive with us tomorrow, but I'm not going to fight with you about it," Anthony said. "Let's go through the security protocol one more time and then you can have the rest of the night with Rowan. That seems to be the most important thing to you."

Quinn answered without hesitation. "It absolutely is."

13

THIRTEEN

Quinn was still grumbling when they returned to the ship, making a series of faces as they readied themselves for bed in Rowan's quarters.

"I never thought of myself as a social person and now I know why. Hanging around with other people is stupid. It's annoying. It's ... really annoying. From now on, I say we tune out the rest of the world and only talk to each another."

Despite her heavy thoughts, Rowan could do nothing but smile. "I think that might get a little weird at a certain point. I mean ... do you really want to talk to me about female stuff?"

Quinn, who was in the middle of tugging off his shirt, stilled. "Define female stuff."

"Well, just off the top of my head, that would include makeup, menstruation, the silly things boys do, my feelings, the little jolt I still get every time I look at you ... oh, and whether or not I want to change my hair."

Quinn smirked at the list. "If you feel a desperate need to talk about makeup with me, I guess I can get behind it."

"And the other stuff?"

"I'm pretending you didn't mention menstruation. I'm a big fan of talking about the jolt you get whenever you see me, though ... mostly because I get the same jolt when I see you. As for your feelings, I want you to discuss those with me, too.

"I get what you're saying, though, and I think it's fine if you want to talk to Sally about makeup and hair," he continued. "I'll take the rest of it on myself. Except for the thing I'm pretending I didn't hear, of course. In my mind that never made the list."

"Good to know," Rowan said dryly, legitimately amused. "As much as I'm glad you're willing to take it on – and I *am* glad – I still think a world where I could only talk to you might strain our relationship a bit. If I can't vent to Sally, that means venting to you and I guarantee you don't want to hear how I hate my new shoes because they pinch."

Quinn pursed his lips. "Okay, but I want you to remember I made this offer the next time Sally takes it upon herself to spread gossip about us."

"She very rarely spreads gossip about us. Also, she never spreads anything hurtful."

"I guess not." Quinn let loose with a sigh as he leaned back on the mattress and stared at the ceiling. "Actually, Sally is on my list of people I like right now. Did I tell you she came to see me the day we were fighting?"

"Yes, and I wouldn't refer to that as fighting. I was pouting and you were apologizing while being wracked with guilt. That's not really fighting."

"It felt like fighting ... and I didn't like it."

"I didn't like it either." Rowan sat at the end of the bed and grabbed Quinn's hand. She'd been considering the best way to bring up the obvious issue for the entire walk back to the ship and had come up with nothing. Everything she thought of seemed awkward and weird. "So ... ."

"You want to ask about the dive." Quinn turned his head and snagged her gaze. "You want to know why I didn't bring it up."

"Are you suddenly a mind reader?" Rowan teased. "Is that what happens when we're the only people in each other's worlds?"

"You're making it into a joke, but it would've benefited both of us tonight. We would've gotten our quiet dinner and time for the Jacuzzi. Instead we had to listen to Anthony and Andrea explain fifty different reasons why they were too cool to get involved."

"Yeah, I think they were protesting a bit much. It's obvious they like each other and are simply making excuses."

"I don't really care about their relationship. I care about our relationship. If you have questions about the dive, though, I would rather you ask them now. I don't want anything festering between us and it's obvious you want to say something about the dive ... so do it."

"Well ... ." Rowan was uncomfortable as she toyed with the bed cover. "When did they offer for you to join them?"

"When they found out about my diving skills," Quinn replied. "Apparently I'm boastful when I'm drunk. My ego must grow with my word-slurring skills."

Rowan snorted. "That sounds feasible. You must have jumped at the chance when they first mentioned it."

"I did."

"And now?"

"I wasn't lying when I said I had things to handle tomorrow."

"See, I think you're covering for me," Rowan hedged. "You don't want me to worry so you're begging off on something that could be legitimately described as a lifelong dream for you."

Quinn purposely kept his expression flat. "Lifelong dream is a bit much."

"Is it?" Rowan quirked an eyebrow. "You've done nothing but talk about The Conqueror since you heard about it. I was trying to think of ways for you to visit when I didn't realize you could dive. I still don't know why I wasn't aware that you could do that ... but we haven't shared every secret with one another so it's nothing to get worked up about.

"You have a chance to see it with your own eyes, though, and I don't want to take that away from you," she continued. "This will be something you'll remember forever. I'm not thrilled about the danger quotient, but I know you'll be careful. I think you should do it."

Quinn worked his jaw as he debated how to respond. "I would be lying if I said I didn't want to see it. The thing is ... I don't want you worried. I don't want to leave you behind. I feel as if I'll be doing something wrong if I do."

"That's a ridiculous thing to think."

"Yeah, but I think it and after what happened ... ."

"What happened was as much my fault as yours," Rowan said after a beat, taking them both by surprise. "I was passive aggressive that night. I sat at the tiki bar and fumed rather than finding you and dragging you away.

"This relationship is still new for both of us and we're testing boundaries, which is normal," she continued. "You can't expect to know every single thing about another person in a few weeks."

"There are times I feel as if I know everything about you," Quinn argued.

"And there are times I feel the same, but it's simply not true. I should've gone to the dining room and collected you. Instead I pouted and felt sorry for myself. That's not the person I want to be. Of course, I also don't want to be the sort of person who makes a scene and drags her boyfriend away when he's having a good time with friends so ... there has to be a happy medium somewhere. I didn't find it that night, but hopefully I will going forward."

"I love how rational your mind is even though you see the fantastical so often." Quinn linked his fingers with Rowan's as he went back to staring at the ceiling. "I do want to dive with them tomorrow."

"Then you should do it."

"I don't want to hurt you."

"It will make me feel worse to think you're giving up a once-in-a-lifetime chance because of me," Rowan said. "I want you to do it. I promise not to melt down. In fact ... I'll go to the dock and wave you off as you head out to sea. That's how much I want you to do it."

Quinn chuckled as he rolled, snagging Rowan around the waist and dragging her to the bed so he could kiss her. The exchange was soft and needy at the same time, and they were both breathless when he raised his head.

"Thank you." His voice was barely a whisper.

Rowan feathered her fingers down his cheek. "Don't thank me. I want this to work for both of us."

"Oh, it's going to work. I have faith. You should, too." And, because he did have faith and wanted to lighten the moment, Quinn started tickling Rowan. She was gasping, tears leaking from her eyes from laughing so hard, when he relented. "Now that I have you at my mercy, there's a different sort of work I'd like us to embrace."

"Somehow that doesn't surprise."

THEY ROSE EARLY, **THE VIEW** from the window still dark. Quinn was playful as they shared a shower, and Rowan knew it was because he wanted her to be at ease when they parted for the day. She was determined to keep her fear to herself, so she encouraged him to expend a bit of energy as they enjoyed their time together.

By the time they got to the dock, Quinn was focused. Rowan had never seen the sort of equipment Andrea surveyed upon their arrival so she couldn't hide her interest.

"What's this?"

"That's a shark spear," Anthony replied, grinning. "We need to fight off the apex predators if we expect to be successful."

Rowan's stomach rolled at his eerie grin. "Oh."

"He's messing with you," Quinn said hurriedly. He recognized the momentary flash on her face for what it was: panic. "There are several types of sharks in this area. The one we'll have a chance of seeing the most of is the reef shark. It's completely harmless."

Rowan was relieved by Quinn's response. "So ... you won't get eaten?"

"No." Quinn shot Anthony a warning look. "Don't mess with her."

"Hey, I'm just glad you're going with us," Anthony said, holding his hands palms up. "I thought for sure your mother would put the kibosh on that."

Rowan wasn't particularly appreciative of being called Quinn's mother, but she managed to bite back a hot retort. Instead she sucked in a steadying breath and offered up a bright smile for Quinn's benefit. "Reef sharks aren't big, right?"

Quinn shook his head. "They're only about six feet or so. They're shy and rarely bother divers. Since there will be so many of us, they'll run in the other direction."

"Yes, the reef sharks are of little concern," Anthony agreed. "I'm more worried about tiger sharks and bull sharks. They're aggressive buggers and far more likely to bite off an arm."

Rowan felt sick to her stomach. "And they'll be down there?"

"Knock it off." Quinn's voice was low and full of warning as he glared at Anthony. "You think it's funny, but I don't. She's never been diving before. She doesn't understand what it's like down there. Freaking her out seems like a particularly cruel thing to do."

Anthony had the grace to look abashed. "That wasn't what I was trying to do."

"That was exactly what you were trying to do," Quinn countered. He tugged a strand of hair behind Rowan's ear and offered up a lopsided grin. "I swear I won't get attacked by a shark. They're not going to be interested in us. All the activity in the area is going to make them want to go someplace else. It's going to be fine."

Rowan nodded. "Okay."

"He's not lying." Anthony adjusted his tone. "I was messing with you. I didn't realize you were legitimately worried. Sharks are not going to be an issue. The shark spears are necessary for insurance reasons and nothing more."

"That makes me feel better." Rowan squeezed Quinn's hand. "So ... you'll be gone all day, right?"

Quinn nodded. "I'll be back in plenty of time for dinner. I promise we'll get our private romantic meal tonight ... even if I have to kill Anthony to do it."

Anthony snorted. "Yeah, yeah."

"What are you going to do all day?" Quinn asked, annoyed he hadn't thought to ask the question earlier.

"I think I'll hang around the island. I might do a little shopping."

"But you'll be alone?"

"I'll be fine." Rowan patted his wrist, amused and touched that he seemed bothered by the prospect. "I managed to survive without your constant companionship before we hooked up. I'll hang around here and shop, maybe get a massage or something."

Quinn didn't look happy at the prospect. "Be careful." He grabbed her purse from her shoulder and slipped it over her head so it couldn't be easily stolen. "Watch your surroundings and don't let strangers crowd you if you can help it."

"Oh, I was wrong," Anthony deadpanned. "You're clearly the mother in this relationship, Davenport."

Quinn ignored him. "Be careful. I'll be home in plenty of time for dinner."

"I'll meet you at my quarters," Rowan suggested.

"Do me a favor," Quinn instructed. "Track down Sally and do your shopping with her. I know I said I wanted us to be the only people in the world last night, but you have fun with her. You can talk about hair ... and makeup ... and that other thing I don't want to talk about."

Rowan giggled at the serious look on his face. "That sounds like a fine idea." She rolled to the balls of her feet and planted a firm kiss on the corner of his mouth. "Have fun. Don't waste your time worrying about me. This is a big deal for you, and I'll feel awful if you don't enjoy it."

"I'll enjoy it." Quinn pressed his hand to the back of Rowan's head and leaned closer. "I'll also enjoy you later. It's going to happen this time. We're taking over that Jacuzzi. I don't care how we do it."

Rowan was delighted as she took a step back. "Make sure you remember everything so you can describe it to me."

"I will. I'll see you soon."

"I'm looking forward to it."

ROWAN WAS SO DETERMINED to enjoy her day she did as Quinn asked. She tracked down Sally and they spent the day shopping and gossiping. For some reason, and Rowan had no idea why, she felt lighter when they were done.

By the time she carried her new possessions back to her quarters, she was weary and considering a nap. Once she woke up, she rationalized, Quinn would be back from his dive and they could have a quiet dinner together where she could share his great day with him.

She settled on the bed, frowning when she noticed the light from her laptop on the nightstand and realized her computer was still on. She'd never shut it down from the previous afternoon. She preferred taking good care of her equipment and silently chided herself for forgetting.

Rowan snagged the laptop and flipped open the screen, widening her eyes when she recognized Quinn's email account popping up rather than her own. That was probably a security no-no, of course. Quinn could get in trouble. Thankfully, Rowan wasn't interested in going through anyone's personal documents.

Something did catch her eye when she moved to close out of the window, though, and she couldn't stop herself from clicking on one of the emails. It was from Fred, and the subject line read "urgent information about Nicholas Green." With a title like that, Rowan rationalized that she couldn't not look.

What she found inside made her wish she'd shown more self-restraint. Her stomach twisted as she read the email, her heart pounding as blood rushed through her ears and threatened to make her go lightheaded.

She read the email three times before she comprehended it, and by the time she was done, a nap was the last thing on her mind.

"I don't believe it."

Rowan was flabbergasted ... and furious. She closed the laptop, leaving it on her bed as she stormed toward the cabin door.

"I can't freaking believe this!"

14

FOURTEEN

Rowan had no idea where she was going. She had no idea where Nick was. She had no idea how to find him so she could confront him. She merely knew she couldn't sit still.

The Bounding Storm was almost completely empty when she hit the main deck. That wasn't surprising. The bulk of the diving team – even those who would be in charge of restoration – were down at the docks waiting to hear back from the first dive crew.

The Bounding Storm's crew was clearly taking advantage of the situation and spending time on El Demonio, which was not only allowed but encouraged to cut down on cabin fever, so that meant Rowan had the run of the ship.

Unfortunately for her, the only thing she wanted to do was run over Nick ... with the biggest truck she could find.

Perhaps it was fate then that she found him after only a brief search.

He stood on the deck, staring out at the island with nothing but a queer look on his face. He seemed lost in thought, perhaps in his own memories, and he didn't hear Rowan approach until she was almost on top of him.

"It's a lovely day," Nick offered, smiling. "I would've thought you'd be on the island."

"I was earlier."

"Did you come back for a specific reason?"

"I went shopping with my friend Sally earlier. I wanted to bring back my things and take a nap."

"It's quiet out here, serene, but you shouldn't sleep in the sun."

"Yes, well, I'm no longer interested in taking a nap." Rowan clenched her hands into fists at her sides. "So … why didn't you tell me you were my uncle from the start?"

Whatever he was expecting, that wasn't it. Nick let the oxygen in his lungs whoosh out as he uttered a strangled gasp. He recovered quickly, although the effort wasn't smooth. "What?"

"Don't bother denying it," Rowan warned, her temper flashing. "I've seen the documents. I know who you are."

Nick licked his lips, giving himself a moment to gather his thoughts. "I see. And what is it that you think you know?"

"You're my father's brother. You're Nick Gray."

"I'm Nick Green," he corrected. "I've been Nick Green for a very long time."

"You were born Nick Gray. Just because you legally changed your name, that doesn't mean you aren't who you were born to be."

"That was a tongue twister, huh?" Nick's expression was bemused. When Rowan didn't crack a smile, he sobered. "You're right. I am your uncle."

Rowan had so many questions fighting for top billing in her head she had no idea where to start. "Why are you here?"

"Perhaps we should find a place in the shade to sit down," Nick suggested kindly. "It's hot. The sun is powerful. This might take a bit of time to explain."

Rowan wanted answers right away, but she nodded. "Fine. We'll go to the tiki bar."

"That's a little more public than I'm comfortable with."

"The ship is empty. We can talk freely there."

"The bartender will be there," Nick pointed out. "You seem friendly with him."

"I am. I'm going to be honest, though. I'm not comfortable being alone with you. It's the tiki bar or nothing."

"Are you sure?" Nick was dubious. "You have a lot of questions. You've always been the curious sort. Something tells me you'll go anywhere with me as long as you think I can fill in some of the gaps for you."

Rowan didn't like his smug expression. "It's the tiki bar or nothing."

"Fine." Nick held up his hands in surrender. "We'll go to the tiki bar. The last thing I want to do is make you feel uncomfortable."

"You should've thought about that before you brought up me being abandoned."

"Was that what led to my downfall?"

"Yes."

"Well, live and learn." Nick heaved out a sigh. "I guess we should get started. This is going to be a very long conversation."

"I KNEW I RECOGNIZED YOU."

Rowan played with the condensation ring left on the tabletop by her glass of iced tea as she stared down Nick. Demarcus hadn't bothered to hide his curiosity when he saw the two of them together, but he wisely left them to their private conversation while remaining behind the bar in case he needed to spring into action and race to Rowan's aid.

For his part, Nick opted for something stronger and sipped a bourbon and water.

"I was around a few times when you were younger," Nick supplied. "Your father and I were closer then and I remember a few rowdy barbecues with your mother's family."

"I don't remember that."

"Perhaps you don't want to remember that."

"And why would that be?"

Nick shrugged, noncommittal. "Maybe your mother's death left you so bereft you forgot the good memories. I can see that happening. You were close with your mother."

"I was close with my father, too," Rowan pointed out. "I don't remember you."

"And yet something inside of you recognized me," Nick pointed out. "I wasn't sure if you would. I was nervous when we were first introduced. I thought you might blurt something out. When you didn't, I relaxed a bit. Of course, part of me was hurt you didn't seem to remember. It was something of a double-edged sword."

"I don't know that I recognized you as much as I felt there was something familiar about you," Rowan corrected. "We saw you at that restaurant the night before we left. I couldn't stop looking at you."

"I saw you, too."

"You acted like you didn't remember seeing me."

"That was part of the game."

"Is that what this is, a game?"

Nick pursed his lips. "No. It's pretty far from a game. Still, when you didn't recognize me right away, I thought it was probably better for you to remain in the dark."

"I don't believe that's true," Rowan argued. "You wouldn't have let the 'abandonment' crack slip if you didn't want to jar my memory. I think you wanted me to be suspicious. I think that's why you kept coming around."

"In truth, I should've stopped talking to you right away and yet I couldn't do it," Nick acknowledged. "You've grown up to be a lovely woman. I see a lot of your mother in you. You have hints of your father, too, though. That's what I most wanted to see."

"If you and my father were so close, why didn't you show up when he disappeared?" Rowan challenged. "Why did you change your name? Why did you show up here?"

"You have a lot of questions. Unfortunately, I'm not sure you'll be happy with my answers."

"Try me."

"Okay." Nick took a long sip of his drink. "Your father and I had a falling out when you were ten. You probably don't remember it, but it was over something stupid."

"When I was ten?" Rowan furrowed her brow. "That was the same year Grandpa died."

"It was." Nick bobbed his head. "That's what we fought about. I wanted to keep Grandpa's house and your father wanted to sell it. Even though I couldn't take care of the house because I was always traveling and the onus of the task would've fallen on your father, I was stubborn and stuck in my ways."

"And that's it?" Rowan felt a bit disillusioned. "That's what you fought about? That's what made you fall out of touch?"

"We didn't fall completely out of touch. I called once a year or so, usually around Christmas. I also sent a gift for you every year, but I'm not sure if you got them. I wasn't a good brother. I was an even worse uncle. Your mother was dead for months before I heard. After that ... after I realized how awful I was ... I was too guilty to call."

"That doesn't make me think you're a good person," Rowan pointed out. "In fact, it makes me dislike you even more. I wasn't sure that was possible until you just said that ... but there it is."

"I don't blame you for disliking me. There's not much to like about what I did. Guilt is a funny thing, though. It makes you introspective. I've spent the better part of the past ten years wishing I had done things differently. I am truly sorry for falling out of touch with your father ... and you. You're my only niece. You're the only family I have left. I should've done so many things differently."

He looked sad and lost, but Rowan refused to let sympathy overtake her. "And after my father disappeared?"

Nick held his hands palms up. "I didn't find out about that until months after it happened either. By then you were ... off on your own."

"You could've called."

"Believe it or not, I went to your house," Nick said. "There was a 'for sale' sign on the lawn and I saw you. I was parked on the street and I watched you carry out a few bags and load them into your car. I was about to get out of my vehicle when you bent over and put your hands on your knees.

"At first I thought you were getting sick," he continued. "Then I realized you were crying. Your shoulders were shaking and your whole body moved with your grief. I felt like an interloper then. A dirty interloper who had no right to interfere with your life."

For some reason, and Rowan didn't know if it was real or imagined, she believed she remembered that exact moment. "You weren't trying to do right by me. You were making things easier on yourself. You didn't want to be the only living family member for an orphaned girl."

Nick's lips twisted. "I wish I could deny that charge. It's ugly and hurtful. It's also the truth. All I could think about when looking at you is that you had no one and I wasn't in a position to be your lone touchstone."

"So you left me alone."

"I did." Nick nodded, offering up a sad chuckle. "I abandoned you and myself at the same time. The guilt was terrible. It ... ravaged me."

"I'm so sorry for *your* loss," Rowan deadpanned. "How difficult it must have been for *you*."

"I don't blame you for being furious. I wouldn't be anything other than irate in your shoes. You have to know, though, that I've thought about you quite often throughout the years. In fact, I've followed your life as closely as possible."

"You've followed my life?"

Nick bobbed his head, warming to the subject. "I kept up with your schooling. I knew when you got a job for the newspaper. I also heard when you lost your job and I was surprised when you showed up on The Bounding Storm.

"I never thought there would be a chance to cross paths with you until this opportunity arose," he continued. "When I realized that we could be on the same ship ... well, I jumped at it. I didn't even need to technically be here and yet I couldn't be anywhere else."

"Is that supposed to make me feel better?" Rowan was proud she managed to keep from bursting into tears. Her insides were raw, somehow weakened by the discovery of her uncle. She remained strong, though. She refused to fall apart. Not now. Not with this man. "You had a chance to watch me up close and personal – perhaps like a trained lab rat – and you couldn't turn away. How great for me, huh?"

"If you wish to yell and scream, that's certainly your prerogative. I've earned your ire."

"You have no idea what you've earned because you weren't around," Rowan exploded, garnering a curious look from Demarcus. She held up her hand to keep him behind the bar, let him know she was okay. She was nowhere near done and she didn't want her personal business spread all over the ship. With that in mind, she adjusted her tone. "I had no one when my father disappeared. I literally had no one. Do you have any idea what that was like for me?"

"I would like to say yes because I'm something of a loner myself, but I know that's not true. You were barely an adult – more of a child really – and you had to grow up on your own. I am so sorry for that. You'll never know how sorry."

"That doesn't do me much good now."

"No, it doesn't," Nick agreed. "The thing is, you grew up to be a strong and wonderful woman. You did all of that on your own. While I'm ashamed that I didn't help you – didn't do something to make what happened easier – I am very proud of how strong you turned out. Your father would be so proud."

Rowan hated the tears pricking the back of her eyes. They didn't make her feel strong. In fact, they made her feel the exact opposite. "Do you know what happened to my father?"

The question caught Nick off guard. "No. Did you think I did?"

"I don't know. I guess I was hoping you did. I mean ... you changed your name. I've always had these wild scenarios flitting through my head that my father had to go on the run because mobsters were after him or something. Changing your name seemed to fit that scenario."

"Ah." Understanding dawned on Nick. "You thought perhaps I helped him escape and had to change my name because of it. Now, ten years after, perhaps it was safe to make contact or something, huh?"

Rowan nodded, her cheeks burning with mortification. "Silly, huh?"

"No, I don't believe that at all." Nick tentatively reached out and awkwardly patted the top of her hand. Rowan didn't jerk away from him, although she didn't look happy at the contact. For now, Nick considered it a win. "I don't know what happened to your father. If it's any consolation – and I don't know if it will make things worse or not – I don't believe he's dead."

Rowan's eyes fired with emotion. "You don't?"

"When I realized I wasn't equipped to help you, I turned my focus to your father," Nick explained. "I wanted to find him for you. I wanted to give you closure. I went in to the investigation thinking that he'd very obviously died and the police simply hadn't found his body yet."

"But?"

"But I looked, sweetheart," Nick said. "I looked far and wide for him. I looked for his car. I looked along any route he could've taken home that day. In fact, I hired divers to search the lake in case he somehow ended up there. That's how I became involved in the diving business in the first place."

"Oh." Rowan had no idea what to make of the admission. "And they didn't find anything?"

Nick shook his head. "They didn't find a single thing."

"And you think that means he's alive?"

"I think that I'm a man of science and without proof of death, I believe he's alive," Nick replied. "I have no idea why he would run, though. I have no idea if he did run. Perhaps someone took him. Perhaps someone forced him to leave."

"He could still be dead then," Rowan pressed. "He could've been taken for some unknown reason and killed after the fact."

"I guess that's true," Nick conceded. "It may be wishful thinking on my part. It might be guilt because I didn't help my niece when I was the only one who could. I'm not sure what it is ... but I believe he's still out there."

Rowan was flummoxed. "I've always wanted to believe that, too. I think people look at me like I'm crazy when I say things like that, though, so I've learned to keep those thoughts to myself."

"You don't have to do that with me."

"Yeah? What is it you want from me?"

Nick's answer was so simple Rowan thought her heart might burst.

"Forgiveness ... and another chance to do right by you."

"Oh, well ... geez."

QUINN WAS **IN A GOOD** mood when he hit The Bounding Storm.

The dive was everything he imagined ... and more. He couldn't wait to share his stories with Rowan. He couldn't wait to tell her about the items they found and what it could mean for future dives.

He paid very little heed to the deck as he moved toward the hallway that led to Rowan's room. He knew she would be there waiting for him and he wanted to see her more than anything.

Quinn had a broad smile on his face when he used his key card to enter her room. Even though it was technically against the rules, he fashioned key cards for her and him so they could freely enter each other's quarters. He told himself it was for simplicity's sake, but it was really a demonstration of trust. He pulled up short when he found the room empty.

"Rowan?" He tilted his head and peered into the empty bathroom, his excitement fading a bit.

The room looked normal other than the laptop sitting on the bed. Rowan usually made sure the computer was tucked away tight before doing anything else. She was almost militant about it.

Out of curiosity, he flipped open the laptop, knitting his eyebrows as he leaned closer and read the open email on the screen. He realized quickly it was from Fred ... and that Rowan must have read it, too. Once he got into the nitty-gritty details, he was flabbergasted.

This couldn't be right. There was no way this was real. And yet ... it seemed to make sense. It explained why Nick was so interested in Rowan, and not in a sexual way. It explained the long stares and constant surveillance.

All of Quinn's earlier excitement dissipated as he realized the ramifications of the discovery. Fury took over, and Quinn was practically vibrating with anger when he straightened.

"Son of a ... ."

15

FIFTEEN

Quinn was relieved when he found Rowan at the tiki bar. The feeling only lasted until he saw who was sitting with her.

He stormed in their direction, his agitation bubbling free, and grabbed Nick by the front of his shirt as he hauled the stunned man to his feet.

"What game are you playing?"

"I'm not playing a game," Nick sputtered. "I ... unhand me."

"Quinn!" Rowan grabbed at her boyfriend's hand in an attempt to get him to loosen his grip. "Let him go."

Quinn slowly turned his attention to Rowan, frustration evident. "You know who he is, right?"

Rowan nodded. "I saw the email. I'm sorry. I should've logged out of your account when I realized it was still up, but I couldn't stop myself from looking."

"Don't apologize." Quinn reluctantly released Nick and ran a hand over his short hair as he fought to calm himself. "I'm not angry about that. I don't blame you for looking. We asked Fred to do the search for your benefit in the first place."

"Yes, well, he came through." Rowan offered up a faux smile that did nothing to brighten her features. "Nick and I have been talking a bit and ... it's complicated."

Quinn's eyebrows winged up. "It's complicated?"

Rowan nodded. "It's all kinds of complicated."

She sank back into her chair. "He's definitely my uncle."

"Well, great." Quinn planted his hands on his narrow hips and glared at Nick. "Welcome to the family. Do you want to explain where you've been for the past ten years?"

Instead of reacting out of fear or anger, Nick merely chuckled. "I like you."

"The feeling isn't mutual."

Nick held up his hand to still Quinn. "You're forceful and brave. You also have strong feelings for my niece. She deserves someone who is willing to fight for her."

"You obviously didn't."

"No, and I'm sorry about that." Nick kept one eye on Quinn as he reclaimed his chair. "We've been discussing my shortcomings as an uncle at length. I'm sure you'll be able to jump right in without a recap."

"You're a funny guy." Quinn took the chair between Rowan and Nick, rubbing his sweaty palms against the front of his shorts as he tried to get comfortable. "Were you this funny when you left Rowan on her own when she was a kid?"

Nick swallowed hard. "I am very sorry for what I did."

"We've talked about it, Quinn." Rowan's voice was low. "He knows he did a bad thing. He had a falling out with my father before then. It's awkward all around."

"That doesn't mean you should simply forgive him."

"No, but ... I don't know." Rowan threw her hands in the air and focused on the string of flamingo lights above the table. "I feel ... overwhelmed."

Quinn's desire to comfort Rowan outweighed his need to slap back Nick further. "Baby ... ." Quinn wasn't a talkative man by nature, but he'd never found himself at a complete loss for words.

"I was thinking that perhaps we could all have dinner tonight," Nick suggested. "I want to get to know Quinn and I would like to reacquaint myself with Rowan now that she's an adult."

"Did you know her as a kid?" Quinn asked the question to buy time. His initial instinct was to snap Nick's neck ... or at least tell him to find another niece whose spirit needed crushing. He wasn't sure that was the right thing for Rowan, though, and he was certain that him taking control of the situation was a bad idea.

"I saw her relatively frequently before she turned ten. After that ... well ... I turned into the world's worst uncle."

"It's hard for us to insult you when you always beat us to the punch," Rowan noted. "As for dinner ... ." She broke off and chewed on her bottom lip as she slid Quinn a sidelong look. "Can you go up and get us refills at the bar, Nick? I would like to talk to Quinn for a few moments in private."

Nick almost looked relieved at the reprieve. "Absolutely. Take your time."

Quinn watched the man scurry toward the bar with a mixture of hatred and disgust. "I can't believe you went through this without me."

Rowan pursed her lips, surprised. "I survived."

"You always do. I should've been here."

"You were dealing with your own adventure. How was the dive, by the way?"

"We'll talk about that later." Quinn was firm. "Right now, I want to talk about this. Do you really want to have dinner with this man? He abandoned you, Ro. He left you alone after you lost both of your parents."

"I know and I don't think what he did was right. More importantly, he doesn't think what he did was right. He's ashamed of how he reacted. He even admitted to watching me in my driveway a few months after my dad disappeared and being too ashamed to get out of the car and talk to me."

"See, that doesn't make me feel better about him. You needed someone ... and he was the only one who could help you. He didn't lift a finger."

"No, but he kept tabs on me. He followed my progress at school and when I started at the newspaper."

"Is that a good thing?"

Rowan shrugged, helplessness and uncertainty ripping through her. "I don't know what you want me to say."

"I want you to tell me what you want. I want to know what will make you happy and then I'll make it happen."

"I don't think that 'happy' is going to play into this. I have to decide if I want to give him another chance and then we'll move forward from there. I don't think anyone is going to be happy simply because I make a decision. It's going to take work either way."

"Not if you shut him out," Quinn countered. "If you turn your back on him like he did with you then you can wash your hands of him."

"Can I?" Rowan wasn't so sure. "Now that I know he's out there and he's been keeping tabs on me, can I just forget and move forward?"

Quinn pressed the tip of his tongue against the back of his teeth. He didn't have an answer.

"Can we at least have dinner with him?" Rowan was embarrassed to ask the question, but she did it all the same. "Can we at least have a meal with him before I decide?"

Quinn nodded without hesitation. He was determined to refrain from making things more difficult for her. "Absolutely. I think that sounds like a good idea. We'll have dinner ... and I have a few questions to ask him."

The way he phrased it caused Rowan to chuckle. "I'll be glad to have you with me this time. I felt as if my brain wasn't working correctly and I can't even remember what I asked the first go around."

"He answered, though, right?"

Rowan nodded. "He was open and flogged himself appropriately."

"Then I'm looking forward to more of that." Quinn grabbed Rowan's hand and gave it a reassuring squeeze. "We're going to get through this. We're going to figure things out. I'm sorry you had to do it alone, though. I mean ... what are the odds?"

"I don't know. Part of me is glad I was alone because it forced me to be strong. The other part is so ridiculously thrilled that you'll be with me for the next leg of questions that I feel a little pathetic."

Quinn leaned forward and rested his forehead against hers, the action intimate and soft. "You're not pathetic. I want to be with you. We'll get through this."

"I know. I think we can get through anything as long we're together. Wait ... did that sound too schmaltzy?"

Quinn grinned as he offered up a quick kiss. "Just schmaltzy enough."

ULTIMATELY THEY SETTLED on a quiet bistro far away from the hustle and bustle of the dock. Quinn was determined to keep things private – for Rowan's sake more than Nick's – and he was relieved to find the restaurant they chose full of locals rather than tourists.

Rowan was so nervous about the meal she changed her outfit four times and took her hair up and down three times before settling on a loose bun. Under different circumstances, Quinn would have found her reaction adorable. Now he could do nothing but share in her anxiety.

They ordered, the two men opting for steak and Rowan going with her seafood standby, before sipping drinks and eyeing each other across the table.

"So, tell me how you two met." Nick's expression was hard to read as he played with the straw wrapper from his drink.

"It was on the ship," Quinn replied. "I ran her background, of course, but we didn't meet in person until she joined the crew."

"Love at first sight?"

Rowan shifted uncomfortably on her chair. "We've only been dating a few weeks."

"Ah, well, you're still close. I like it."

"How about you?" Quinn challenged. "Why did you change your name?"

Rowan knew the meal wouldn't be easy, but she almost choked at the abrupt question as she sipped her cocktail.

"Honestly? I felt guilty," Nick replied. "I felt guilty for walking away from my brother and not being there when his wife was sick and dying. Then I felt even more guilty because I thought I was going to help Rowan, but I ran away a second time. I wanted a fresh start."

"No, you wanted to make it so she couldn't track you down," Quinn corrected. "You were afraid she would find you one day and call you on your crap."

"Quinn." Rowan's voice was low and full of warning. "Please don't do ... that."

Quinn spared her a glance. "Ro, I feel the need to ask him direct questions. You're my primary concern. That means he's now a big concern, only of a different kind."

"He has a right to ask the question," Nick said, waving off Rowan's protests. "I don't blame him. I'm not the good guy in your story. I'll never be the hero who swooped in and saved you from difficulty."

Rowan scratched at her cheek. "Really? Because I was thinking about something when I was getting ready for dinner and I have a question to ask you."

"I told you to ask any questions you want."

"Okay." Rowan licked her lips. "When I was a senior in college, I almost ran out of money to complete my course load before graduation. I worked hard and kept my nose to the grindstone, but there was a time when I thought I would have to drop out because classes were more expensive than I envisioned.

"I was upset because I knew I would never have the chance to go back," she continued. "My mother always wanted me to go to college because she never got the chance. Part of me was desperate to live up to what I thought she wanted.

"Out of nowhere, like two days before my final semester, I got word that I earned a scholarship I never applied for," she said. "I remember thinking it was a miracle. That somehow my mother did something from Heaven to save me.

"Now, I don't know why, but while I was showering, the name of the company that gave me that scholarship popped into my mind." Rowan's gaze was steady on Nick. "It was the Green Technology Group. I sent a thank-you note to the address listed on the paperwork but never heard anything else from them."

Nick pressed the heel of his hand to his forehead. "I still have the note you sent. For a time I told myself you sent it directly to me as an uncle, even though I knew better."

"I knew it." Rowan shook her head, dumbfounded. "You sent that money."

"I did. I was in contact with the school at times to make sure you would be able to stay. I absorbed any additional dorm fees and as many classroom fees as I could. I believe you won free meals for life while at school through a raffle, too. I should point out that's a raffle that doesn't technically exist."

Rowan's mouth dropped open. "That was you, too?"

"I wanted to help and yet I was terrified of seeing you." Nick's guilt was palpable. "I was a weak man and it made me feel better to know that you were strong, that you would overcome. That's the best legacy your parents could leave you with."

"Oh, man." Quinn slapped his hand to his forehead, disgusted.

"Too much?" Nick was genuinely amused.

"No. Now I simply can't hate you as much as I wanted to hate you." Quinn slung his arm over the back of Rowan's chair. "If you were so afraid to see her, why did you come on this trip? You had to know Rowan was on The Bounding Storm."

"I did know that," Nick confirmed. "I didn't have to come. I could've coordinated from the Florida office. That's where I'm based now."

"But?"

"But I couldn't stop myself from taking the chance," Nick replied. "She's my only living relative. Er, well, I have some cousins scattered across the country, but they don't count. Rowan is the last link I have to my brother."

"And what did you think when you first saw her?" Quinn asked.

"That she looked like a beautiful mix of her parents."

"After that."

"That I couldn't decide if I was happy or sad that she didn't recognize me," Nick answered truthfully. "Part of me wanted her to throw her arms around my neck and welcome me onboard. The other part was terrified she would slap me across the face and tell me never to bother her again."

"I would've been all for the second one," Quinn said dryly. "Still, you took a big chance. You took an even bigger one baiting her with the stuff you knew about her past."

"Yes, well, it seems my wits ran for the hills as soon as I was face to face with her," Nick noted. "I can't explain it."

"I can." Quinn was matter-of-fact. "I think you wanted her to know who you were and your subconscious wouldn't leave it alone. You kept pushing and pushing ... ultimately recognizing that she would push back."

"I guess that's possible," Nick hedged. "It makes me sound a bit diabolical, though."

"I haven't ruled out that possibility." Quinn traced a lazy pattern of circles on the back of Rowan's neck as she watched the exchange. "If you want to make things up to Rowan, I think you're going to have a long road ahead of you. It's not my place to say it – and yet I'm going to anyway. Don't even start going down the road if you're going to turn tail and run again. That will make things worse."

"Is that what you think I'm going to do?"

"I don't know," Quinn replied. "I don't want her hurt. If you hurt her, I'm going to hurt you."

Instead of balking at the threat, Nick chuckled. "Son, I don't want to hurt her. I don't want to run any longer either. I'm too old for that. I'd like to find a happy middle ... a place where we can all coexist."

Quinn slid his eyes to Rowan and found her staring at her uncle with rapt attention. "Then we'll figure it out."

Nick's smile was so grateful that Quinn had to force himself to remain edgy rather than softening.

"We'll figure it out," Rowan echoed, bobbing her head. "So ... how do we start?"

"I believe we start with a simple conversation," Nick said. "So, with that in mind ... tell me about the dive today, Quinn. I haven't had a chance to touch base with anyone on my team so your report is the first I'm hearing."

This time the smile on Quinn's face wasn't purely for Rowan's benefit. He leaned back in his chair, keeping his arm around Rowan, and launched into the tale of his afternoon. In the grand scheme of things, Rowan found it all a little boring. She would never say that to Quinn, though, because he clearly had the time of his life.

When he was done with the story, Quinn was more relaxed and Nick was intrigued.

"So they found a few coins?"

Quinn nodded. "They didn't look like coins to me because there was so much other stuff attached to them, but the restoration team was excited and they took the relics straight back to the ship to treat."

"Well, that's something." Nick rolled his neck. "This entire endeavor has been something of a leap of faith. I'm happy to see that it appears to be working out."

"Didn't you think it would?" Rowan asked. "I mean ... isn't this what you expected to find?"

"Yes and no," Nick replied. "The Conqueror was thought lost at sea a long time ago. Technically, we haven't confirmed that's what we found. So far we only have a shipwreck that seems to date to Revolutionary War times."

"But I thought it was confirmed," Rowan countered, wrinkling her forehead.

"It's been confirmed as much as possible," Nick supplied. "It's not as if we're going to find the captain and confirm it. This find could be worth a great deal of money, though. That's what concerns me most."

"Isn't the money good for you?"

"Yes, but there are a lot of different factions trying to lay claim to the money," Nick explained. "We won the bid for the initial dive and restoration, but who knows how long that will last. Plus, well, whenever something like this occurs there seems to be a race to see who can profit first."

"But you have permits, right?" Quinn asked.

"We do. Permits won't stop thieves from trying to take advantage of the situation."

"You seem really worried," Rowan noted. "It won't get dangerous, will it?"

"I certainly hope not," Nick replied. "I'm not ruling anything out. Still, though, as fascinating as the dive is, I would like to talk about you. I want to know how you've found life onboard The Bounding Storm ... and I would like to know how you guys decided to start dating. Something tells me that's going to be a fascinating story."

Quinn chuckled. "I think that depends on who you ask. Everyone we know thinks we're boring."

"I doubt very much that's the truth."

Quinn wasn't about to be deterred. "Don't say I didn't warn you."

SIXTEEN

"How are you feeling?"

Quinn put his hand to Rowan's back as they hit the hallway and turned toward the main dining room the next morning.

They'd stayed up late into the night talking to Nick, going for ice cream after dinner and indulging in a few stories from Rowan's childhood that appealed to Quinn because she rarely offered up good memories with her mother and father. Everything for Rowan turned bad with death and disappearance, and it was almost as if she didn't remember the good times. Quinn was glad to see that Nick could bring out her laughter, which almost sounded childlike because it was so light.

It was nearly midnight before they returned to the ship and parted ways. Quinn's hope for private time in the high-rollers' Jacuzzi was shoved off for another night, but he was fine with it because Rowan seemed so happy when they climbed into bed together.

She remained happy the next morning, and Quinn was grateful to see the smile on her face when she looked to him.

"I feel good. I have a bit of a sugar hangover from the ice cream, but I'm sure that will fade when I get some real food into me."

"I'm looking forward to real food, too." Quinn's fingers were flat on the small of Rowan's back as they walked. "While I was glad for some privacy, that wasn't the best meal I've ever had."

"The scallops were kind of rubbery."

"I'm pretty sure the steak wasn't beef."

Rowan snorted, the sound warming Quinn. "Well, thank you for sitting through the meal. I know it was hard for you. If you would've gotten food poisoning on top of everything else, I would've felt guilty."

"You have no reason to feel guilty." Quinn meant it. "Ro, I wanted to be there with you. I wouldn't have it any other way. In fact, I feel a little guilty because I wasn't with you when you found out. I can't help but think I should have been there."

"There's no way you could have known. Beating yourself up over it does no one any good. I wasn't lying when I said I was glad to face Nick on my own, at least at the first. I was also really glad you were there for dinner because I was so nervous I thought I might pass out."

"I never would've noticed," Quinn teased, pressing a kiss to the tender spot behind her ear. "Still, I'm glad you got a chance to sit down with him. Despite what he did, he doesn't seem like a bad guy."

"Before you showed up yesterday, he said something that kind of stuck with me," Rowan admitted. "He said that the longer he stayed away, the easier it was to come up with excuses. Then, when it came time to come back, he'd left it so long he couldn't bring himself to right certain wrongs and he spent all of his time wallowing in fear and regret."

"Did he use the word 'wallow'?"

"I might've added that."

"Yeah, that's totally a chick word." Quinn smirked as he held open the dining room door so Rowan could squeeze in ahead of him. "Still, I get what he's saying. That doesn't mean what he did is okay."

"He doesn't think it's okay."

"He doesn't, which is the only reason I haven't popped him in the face."

Quinn followed Rowan to the buffet line, watching with a mixture of baffled amusement and disbelief as she piled enough food on her plate to feed three people. "Hungry?"

"I'm starving," Rowan admitted. "Dinner last night was bad and I was so nervous I'm not sure I could've eaten more than I did anyway. Plus, the added sugar from those huge cones we got made me a bit jittery."

Quinn chuckled. "Well, you should be able to balance your blood sugar on that. Pancakes, eggs, French toast, hash browns, corned beef hash, bacon, and sausage? I think you're going to take the world's longest nap this afternoon after eating all that."

"I'm hungry. Sue me."

"Hey, I'm happy to see it." Quinn added much smaller portions to his plate as he trailed her through the line. "Speaking of Nick, have you decided if you're going to tell anyone who he really is?"

Rowan shook her head. "I think it's too soon. I don't want to deal with it. People don't understand what happened with my father. Heck, I don't understand what happened with my father. Trying to explain this to other people seems ... well ... let's just say I don't want to be one of those annoying women who shares every single facet of her life with virtual strangers at the hair salon."

"I'm not sure I know exactly what that means, but I get your drift," Quinn said. "What do you plan to do today? Are you going to spend time with Nick?"

Rowan nodded. "We're having breakfast with him."

Quinn stilled. "We are?"

Rowan gestured toward a corner table with her shoulder. Nick was already seated and sipping coffee. "He asked last night when you were throwing away the wrappers from the ice cream cones. I agreed. Now I'm starting to think I probably should've run it by you first."

Quinn immediately started shaking his head. "No. It's fine. I want you to spend as much time with him as you're comfortable with as long as he's on the ship. It's not as if he's going to be here forever."

"No," Rowan agreed. "He lives in Florida, though. I asked specifically where and he said Miami. When we're docked, that's not too far from us."

Quinn practically read her mind. "And we can set up meals with him whenever you want. In fact ... now that I know he's not a demented pervert ... you can probably do stuff with him alone if you want, too."

Rowan snickered. "Thank you so much for your permission."

Quinn refused to be baited into an argument due to her tone. "You're welcome."

The duo cut their way across the dining room, largely ignoring the bulk of the workers who were excitedly talking about the previous day's finds. By the time they joined Nick, the older man's face was practically swallowed by a huge smile.

"I see you still have the same appetite you had as a kid," Nick noted, staring at Rowan's plate. "Are you really going to eat all of that?"

Rowan shrugged. "I'm hungry."

"You certainly didn't eat much last night," Nick said, smiling as Quinn took the spot across from him. "How was the rest of your evening?"

"Quiet," Quinn replied. "We went straight to bed."

"Oh, no!" Rowan's hand flew to her mouth. "We missed your Jacuzzi trip again. I completely forgot."

Quinn chuckled dryly. "I'll try not to take it personally. It's fine, though. We have plenty of time to hit the Jacuzzi. You were so exhausted when we got back you were already snoring by the time I finished brushing my teeth."

Rowan balked. "I don't snore."

"Then you must have been doing a very impressive impersonation of someone who does snore."

Rowan turned to Nick for support. "I don't snore."

"Your father used to snore like a freight train," Nick said. "I know because we shared a room for what felt like forever. If you do snore, I'm sure you come by it honestly."

Rowan was appalled. "I don't snore." She viciously stabbed her fork into a sausage link. "I don't."

Quinn took pity on her. "They were lovely and delicate female snores, Ro. It sounded more like angels singing than snoring."

Rowan rolled her eyes as Nick loudly guffawed.

"Oh, you're just placating me," Rowan complained.

"You're still cute when you sleep." Quinn squeezed her shoulder before turning his attention to Nick. Under normal circumstances, he would be embarrassed to talk about sleeping in the same bed with a woman when her uncle was present. Since Nick was sort of a new uncle, Quinn refused to be uncomfortable and instead met the man's steady gaze with a half-smile. "What's the plan for today?"

"I heard you were going diving with Andrea's team again," Nick said. "That's what she told me over our planning session this morning."

"You've already had a planning session?" Rowan was impressed as she chewed her pancakes. "All we've done is get up and shower."

"Yes, well, we need to talk about what was discovered yesterday and there's been some discussion of gridding the search area," Nick explained. "The thing is, because the wreck has been there for so long, we're looking at a couple of scenarios."

"Like what?" Rowan sipped her tomato juice.

"How come you're not this interested when I talk about shipwrecks?" Quinn teased.

"I am as long as you're shirtless," Rowan fired back. "I'm honestly interested in what's going on. I want to hear ... no matter which one of you explains things."

"I think I'll leave it to Nick this morning so I can watch you stuff your face," Quinn said as he used his napkin to dab at the corner of Rowan's mouth. "If I steal one of your bacon slices, are you going to go all growly and smack me around?"

"You wish."

Quinn snatched some bacon and turned his eyes to Nick. "We're listening. She just needs to eat while she's doing it."

Nick chuckled, amusement evident. "I like how happy you two are. It lightens the weight on my shoulders. I can't tell you how much. Anyway, as for The Conqueror, we have no idea if that's where the ship actually went down. That makes things more difficult."

"I thought you found the ship, though."

"We found certain things," Nick hedged. "We found some cannons, although we've been unable to drag those up yet and only one looks to be in salvageable shape. In fact, I'm taking the submersible down myself this afternoon so I can get a better look at what we're dealing with."

"A sub?" Rowan perked up.

"A submersible," Nick corrected. "It's much smaller than a sub. We don't have to go really deep, so the submersible is fine ... and you don't have to get wet to enjoy the view. It's big enough to fit five or six people comfortably, although there will be nowhere near that number today."

"Well, that sounds fun. Go back to what you were saying about not knowing exactly where The Conqueror went down. How could the cannons be here and not the ship?"

"I can take that," Quinn offered, not waiting for a response. "There are several scenarios here, Ro. The first is that The Conqueror went down during a storm and broke apart at sea. That means the cannons could've landed one place, the internal furnishings another, and the gold hold even another."

"You see, if the ship broke apart, the two halves could be miles apart," Quinn added.

"Another scenario is that The Conqueror went down farther out and the tide moved the wreckage throughout the years," Quinn said. "Underwater currents are strong – especially in this area – and you would be surprised how quickly tides could change the landscape."

"How so?" Rowan asked.

"Say the ship only moved fifty to a hundred feet each year underwater," Nick offered. "That wouldn't look like much to the naked eye and is entirely possible. Now do the math. If the ship moved a hundred feet a year and it's been more than two hundred years ... ."

"I see what you're saying." Rowan switched to her scrambled eggs. "The Conqueror could've gone down much farther out and then migrated closer."

"Yes. Like I said, the tides are strong."

Rowan turned her inquisitive eyes to Quinn. "Is that what you think happened?"

"I honestly don't know," Quinn replied. "I didn't see any of the cannons yesterday. That was Anthony. He was excited when we hit the dock, but I didn't hang around too long because I wanted to check on you."

"We want to find a way to bring at least one of them up," Nick said. "That's why I'm going down in the submersible. Anthony recommended I see it with my own eyes, because it's not an easy task."

"All of this is above my paygrade," Rowan noted. "You said last night, though, that there are multiple factions interested in finding The Conqueror's haul. Is that because of the gold that was supposedly on board?"

"The Conqueror was mostly filled with soldiers and weapons," Nick clarified. "There was some money, although what that money was for remains a mystery."

"I don't understand."

"Some people thought the money was meant as a payoff to the American colonists," Quinn explained. "The money was to be used for goods, services, and soldier payments."

"Other people believe the money was for bribes to British officers," Nick added. "The entire thing was all very ... mixed up. I guess that's the right way to put it. No one really knew why the money was on board."

"But it's important because it's worth so much now, right?" Rowan pressed. "Whoever finds the money – whether it be coins or gold – is looking at a windfall, aren't they?"

"In theory," Nick answered. "There is still some debate about who gets what. I'm more interested in the history than anything else, but I would like to see the coins and gold myself. That's obviously the big draw for my employers."

"So what's the problem?" Rowan asked. "You said they found coins yesterday."

"They did." Nick bobbed his head. "The fact that the coins are strewn around means we're probably not going to find everything in one spot. That complicates matters."

Rowan turned to Quinn. "Do you know what he's saying?"

"Obviously the hope was to find a big pile of coins sitting out in the middle of the ocean just waiting to be claimed," Quinn said. "If they're strewn about, the operation is going to take a lot longer than a week."

"Oh." Things clicked into place for Rowan. "If you don't find more soon, then we'll leave you here and you'll continue on with a different group ... and a different plan."

"Kind of," Nick hedged. "I don't have to stay here. I can and will go back to Florida within about a week or so. You don't have to worry about us not seeing each other right away, so don't fret about that."

Rowan was sheepish. "Was I that obvious?"

Quinn snickered. "I thought it was cute."

"You supposedly think the snoring is cute, too."

"I stand by my earlier statement."

"A longer dive simply means more headaches," Nick explained. "The longer things drag out, the more likely that there will be infighting regarding the find. It would be easier – for me, at least – if we found more items ... and fast."

"And you're going diving again?" Rowan asked Quinn.

"I was going to but wanted to talk to you first. If you don't want me to ... ."

"I think you should go. This isn't something you're going to be able to do a second time. You should enjoy it while you can."

Quinn spared a glance for Nick. "I'm not comfortable leaving you alone for the entire day, Ro. Not again."

"She won't be alone," Nick said. "In fact, I was going to bring it up earlier, but we got sidetracked. I think what I have to offer will be a nice compromise, though."

"And what's that?" Quinn asked, interested despite himself.

"I have a submersible," Nick reminded him. "Rowan can come down with me. That way she'll be able to see what we're looking at, see the things you see, and be perfectly safe at the same time."

Rowan straightened her shoulders. "Seriously?"

Nick chuckled. "I don't see why not."

Rowan looked to Quinn. "What do you think?"

"I actually like the idea a great deal," Quinn replied after a beat. "It's not so deep it's dangerous. You'll be safe inside the submersible and won't have to worry about the tide or anything. I'll be close and know where you are. I also won't have to describe everything I've been seeing. Trust me. It loses something in the telling."

"And I can really go with you?" Rowan was wide-eyed and excited, her breakfast all but forgotten.

"I'm the boss," Nick said. "Of course you can go."

"Well ... yippee." Rowan speared another sausage link, this time with excitement rather than embarrassment. "My day is looking up."

Quinn and Nick exchanged amused glances.

"I was thinking the same thing," Quinn said. "It's going to be an exciting day for all of us."

SEVENTEEN

"What's going on?"

Rowan and Quinn met a group of divers – including Andrea and Anthony – at the front of the ship before heading toward the dock. It was obvious something had happened, although what was anybody's guess.

"One of our divers is missing," Anthony replied, making an annoyed face.

Quinn's eyebrow winged up. "Missing? When was the last time anyone saw him? Wait ... is it a him?"

Anthony nodded. "Stuart Dombrowski. He was at that bar on the island last night, the one with the ... um ... specialized dancers." His cheeks colored as he spared a glance for an approaching Nick. "I saw him there myself right around midnight and told him to come back to the ship and get some sleep. He said he was going to, but apparently he didn't."

Quinn gave him a quick rundown before focusing on Anthony. "Are you sure he didn't come back?"

"We checked his room. We thought maybe he was up here, but obviously not."

"Could something have happened to him?" Nick was calm. "I mean ... could he have fallen in with the wrong sorts at the bar last night? You said there were dancers. What kind of dancers?"

Rowan took pity on her uncle. "The kind who lose their costumes as the night progresses," she supplied. "At least that's what I think they're referring to."

"That would be the one," Anthony confirmed.

"Do we have any reason to believe he's met with foul play?" Nick's eyes were on Quinn when he asked the question.

"I don't think so," Quinn replied. "I think it's far more likely that he hooked up with someone and lost track of time."

"Which puts us in an interesting position," Nick noted. "Okay, we'll give it the day. If we return to The Bounding Storm and he still hasn't come back, we'll alert local authorities. If he does come back on his own, I expect him to be removed from the team." His gaze was pointed when it landed on Andrea. "He's your man, but he clearly can't be trusted."

Andrea balked. "He was simply blowing off steam."

"This is an important find," Nick reminded her. "I have no problem with divers blowing off steam. I do have a problem with them shirking their duties. I expect you to deal with this when he turns back up, Andrea. It's your team."

Andrea nodded curtly. "I'll handle it."

"Great." Nick turned his focus to Anthony. "I will be going down in the submersible today. I want to see the cannon you found and scope the site. We'll discuss the best way to get the cannon up this afternoon."

"That sounds like a plan." Anthony beamed as he flicked his eyes to Rowan. "Are you going to join us today? I can't say I won't enjoy seeing you in a wetsuit."

Quinn made a growling sound as he glared.

"I was just kidding," Anthony added hurriedly. "You need to learn to lighten up a bit."

"Ms. Gray is going in the submersible with me," Nick supplied.

"I want her to take photos of the site. I think they'll be a nice conversation piece when we're finished."

"She's going to take photos from inside the submersible?" Anthony was perplexed. "Won't those turn out ... um ... ugly?"

Now it was Rowan's turn to make a face. "They'll be great. Don't worry about it."

Anthony held up his hands in mock surrender. "I wasn't trying to offend you."

"Your mouth is just all over the place this morning," Quinn grumbled, shaking his head. "Have you ever considered not talking?"

Anthony's lips curved. "What fun would that be?"

"A lot for the rest of us. Let's get going. We're burning daylight and an undersea adventure awaits." Quinn held out his hand to Rowan. "You're about to see a whole new world, Ro. I think you're going to like it."

"Is it wrong that I'm excited?" Rowan asked, giddy.

"Not even a little. I'm excited for you."

"THIS IS **A LOT** smaller space than I was expecting."

Rowan glanced around the tiny submersible – it wasn't much bigger than the bathroom and closet combo in her quarters, which was tiny – and did her best to tamp down the claustrophobic feelings threatening to overwhelm her.

"I told you." Nick watched Rowan's busy eyes with a smirk. "You'll be fine. Just remember we're not going so far beneath the surface that you're in any danger."

Rowan wasn't convinced that was true. "What happens if this thing stops working?"

"Then we would call for aid and the ships on the surface would raise the sub."

"Oh." That was an easier answer than Rowan was expecting. "What happens if they can't raise it?"

"Then we would have to put on diving gear and head to the surface ourselves."

"Is that something we'd be capable of doing?" Rowan challenged. "I mean ... what if the big window cracked and water started seeping in? What would happen to us then?"

Nick fixed Rowan with an amused look. "How would the window crack? We're not at crush depth."

"No, but ... what if a shark decided to ram his head into the window and cracked it?"

"I believe you watch too many movies," Nick said dryly. "You clearly inherited that from your father. When we were kids, he used to come up with elaborate scenarios like the one you just whipped out for no apparent reason. It used to drive me crazy."

Rowan spared a glance at the captain of the submersible, but he was in his own little box and sported a pair of headphones as he focused on his job. "Can he ... ?"

"If he wants, but that's Larry Danes. He doesn't care for gossip so he'll tune us out. That's why I picked him for this particular trip."

"Oh." Rowan settled, if only marginally. "So we're not in any danger of dying, right?"

Nick tried to bite back a chuckle ... and failed miserably. "You're not in any danger of dying. I wouldn't have invited you if I thought that was the case."

"Okay, well ... ." Rowan leaned back in her chair, forcing a nonchalant look as she rested her hands on her knees. "So ... do you come here often?"

Nick's chuckle was so loud and warm it reminded Rowan of her father. The realization was enough to jolt her, and when she looked to her uncle she had tears in her eyes.

"What's wrong?" Nick instantly sobered and reached for her hand. "If you're afraid, I can have the submersible turned around and take you back to the dock."

Rowan shook her head. "I'm not afraid. You just reminded me of

Dad when you laughed like that. He used to do the same thing when he thought I said something especially goofy."

Nick relaxed his shoulders, his smile watery. "Your father loved you a great deal."

"Not enough to stay," Rowan pointed out. "Do you think he's really out there somewhere?"

"I do, but I wish I hadn't told you that."

"Why?"

"Because it's clearly given you hope ... and an insecurity complex. I don't want you questioning your father's love for you. It's cruel and I'm sorry you're going through it."

"But if he left ... ."

"He might not have had a choice," Nick pointed out. "We have no idea what was going on with him at the time of his disappearance."

"Yes, but you would think that he would've told me if there was something wrong," Rowan pressed. "You would think that he would've found a way to reach out to me if he were still alive ... even if only to put my mind at ease."

"You would think." Nick ran an affectionate hand down the back of Rowan's head. "Like I said yesterday, I believe your father is alive. I have faith. As for the other stuff ... I guess we'll need to wait until that works itself out."

Rowan wrinkled her nose. "That was an odd way to phrase it."

"I'm an odd guy." Nick offered up a playful wink before pointing. "We're getting closer to the ocean bottom. Now you can see what we're dealing with."

Rowan snapped her head to the window, abandoning the conversation about her father and focusing on an entirely new world. "Look at that." She leaned forward, practically pressing her face against the window and openly gaped at the sights. "It's like a movie."

"It's better than a movie," Nick countered. "It's real ... and it's magical."

"It really is." Rowan didn't care that the bottom of the submersible was probably dirty. She didn't care that she possibly looked like a loon when she pressed her forehead to the window. All she cared about was the seemingly magical world on the other side of the glass. "This is ... unbelievable."

Nick watched her rather than the scene unfolding in the ocean. "I'm glad you're here. It's more fun seeing it with you."

Rowan smiled, although she didn't move her eyes from the window. "I'm glad you're here, too. This is just ... amazing. I'll never forget this moment."

Nick chuckled. "Me either."

AN HOUR LATER, **ROWAN'S** enthusiasm was still rampant, but she managed to collect herself long enough to snap some photos. The glass on the front of the submersible was clear so she had no problem grabbing a series of beautiful shots.

"There's Quinn." She pointed, excited, when a figure in a wetsuit turned in their direction and waved.

"How can you be sure that's him?" Nick asked, genuinely curious. "Does he wave a certain way?"

Rowan shook her head. "He carries himself a certain way, though. I can just tell it's him."

Nick watched her as she waved back at the man in the water, enjoying the way her face lit up when Quinn moved closer to the submersible's window and pressed his hand to the other side of the glass. They weren't sharing the same oxygen and yet they were participating in something wonderful ... together.

"You love him," Nick noted, smiling as Quinn swam off to begin his search.

Rowan balked. "We haven't been dating that long. I told you that last night."

"That doesn't mean you don't love him," Nick argued. "Sometimes the greatest loves are the ones that hit us over the head and take over our lives out of nowhere."

Rowan turned a curious look to her uncle. "Have you loved like that?"

"No, but I know others who have."

"I've been trying to remember the time before Mom died," Rowan said. "It's not easy because I purposely shut out a lot of those memories."

"Because it hurt too much to remember?"

Rowan shrugged. "Because it was easier to forget. At least that's why I think I did it. Remembering made me sad and, at a certain point, if I got any sadder I think it would've been the end for me."

Nick licked his lips, tilting his head to the side as he considered the statement. "What do you mean by that?" he asked finally, gently. "Did you ever consider ... ?"

Rowan vehemently shook her head. "No. Not really. I never thought of killing myself or anything. There were days I didn't want to get out of bed, though. A few times, there were a few days in a row. I recognized the danger in that so I forced myself to stop thinking about the past and look toward the future.

"All I could do was put one foot in front of the other and keep marching," she continued. "Sometimes I think I was going through the motions, but it kept me sane. It helped me get here."

"And are you happy here?"

Rowan's smile lit up her entire face. "I am. What's not to be happy about? I live on a cruise ship. My boyfriend is smoking hot and always willing to listen to what I have to say. I have friends. I found you. Things are better than they've been since ... well, since I was a kid."

"I'm glad." Nick said the words and his expression reflected the truth behind them. "I want you to be happy more than anything else."

"I'm happy." Rowan lifted her camera and snapped several photos through the glass, focusing on a group of divers near a cluster of coral. "I'm so happy I'm going to be able to focus on finding a girlfriend for you once we get into a routine after this trip."

Nick snorted. "I believe I can find my own girlfriend."

"You haven't done it yet."

"I have other things on my mind. More important things."

"Like?"

"Like you," Nick replied without hesitation. "Once I found out there was a chance I would be able to see you in person, that's all I could think about. I also have to deal with this."

Nick gestured toward the expansive undersea world. "Do you see that over there?"

Rowan followed his finger with her eyes. "What? That oddly-shaped reef? Yeah, I see it."

"That's not just a reef," Nick explained. "Oh, don't get me wrong, it is a reef now. It wasn't always a reef, though."

"What was it?"

"Part of The Conqueror."

Rowan narrowed her eyes, dumbfounded. "But ... how?"

"Nature always finds a way," Nick explained. "You look at this spot and see beauty. It's all natural beauty to you, though. I see what once was ... and know I somehow need to find what's hidden beneath the beauty."

"Huh. I never really considered that before." Rowan rolled her neck before taking a few shots of the reef. "You really know your stuff."

Nick chuckled dryly. "It's been a learning endeavor, but I enjoy my job."

"I enjoy mine, too," Rowan said, pulling back so she could stare at the viewfinder on the back of the camera. "I've loved taking photos since Dad first put a camera in my hand. It just felt ... right."

"Yes, I remember the little one you had when you were ten. You were adorable with it. Sure, you were kind of annoying because you kept sticking it in people's faces, but you were adorable all the same."

"Yeah." Rowan's full attention was on the back of her camera and it took Nick a moment to realize she'd dropped out of the conversation.

"Do you see something?" Nick asked.

"Um ... ." Rowan wasn't sure how to answer. Her heart hammered so hard she briefly thought there was a chance she would pass out. She wouldn't allow that, though, instead leveraging all her focus on the photograph.

Nick furrowed his brow. "What do you see?"

"Um ... ." Rowan was flustered. Now didn't seem the time to bring up her special ability. She couldn't simply ignore it either. "Well ... can you get in contact with the divers?"

"I can," Nick confirmed, his expression thoughtful. "You see it, don't you?"

Rowan balked. "See what?"

"The omen."

Rowan was flabbergasted. "How can you possibly know about that?"

"I know a lot more than you give me credit for," Nick replied calmly. "Your father mentioned your ability before we had our falling out."

Rowan did the math in her head. "That can't be right."

"Show me," Nick prodded, moving closer. "Show me what you see."

Rowan pointed to a spot on the digital image. After a long beat, Nick saw what she was referring to.

"That's it?"

Rowan chewed on her bottom lip as she nodded. "She's going to die. You probably don't believe that but ... ."

"You would be surprised what I believe." Nick rested his hand on Rowan's shoulder to steady her. "Don't worry. I've got everything under control. I'll get her out of the water. In fact ... I'll get them all out of the water."

"I'm pretty sure this is Andrea," Rowan noted. "I can't see her face up close, but I recognize the hair."

"I believe you're right." Nick rolled his neck as he reached for his radio. "Don't worry. We'll get them out."

"What are you going to say?" Rowan was understandably nervous. "You're not going to tell them about me, are you?"

"Of course not." Nick shook his head. "There's a reason you keep your ability secret. There's also a reason you should keep hiding it. Only tell those you trust completely. As for this, I'm in charge. I can do whatever I want.

"Trust me," he continued, rolling his neck. "I've got everything under control. You don't have to worry about anyone finding out your secret. I won't let it happen. That's one thing you can always rely on me for."

18

EIGHTEEN

"What's going on?"

Anthony's agitation was evident as he stalked toward Nick once everyone regrouped on the dock.

Quinn, perhaps sensing trouble, smoothly stepped in front of Rowan. The move wasn't lost on Nick, and if the man didn't already like his niece's boyfriend, he would be absolutely over the moon about him now.

"I wanted to talk strategy," Nick said calmly, his eyes landing on a confused-looking Andrea. "In fact, it's close enough to lunch that I thought we would order something delivered here and come up with a plan to lift the cannon."

Rowan was confused. She didn't even remember seeing the cannon. Of course, Nick was doing all of this to protect her so she couldn't very well call him to task in front of witnesses.

"That could've waited an hour," Anthony pressed. "You didn't have to pull us up early."

"And yet I did." Nick refused to be pulled into an argument. "We'll meet at that group of picnic tables over there in thirty minutes to discuss our next step. I'll order food."

"That's it?" Anthony was incensed, something Rowan didn't understand.

"That's it," Nick confirmed, turning his back to Anthony and fixing Quinn with a pointed look. "You know the area relatively well, right? Perhaps you can help me pick a restaurant."

Quinn was too smooth – and smart – to offer up an argument. "That sounds fine."

Nick led the way toward a spot in the shade, Quinn and Rowan following. No one questioned why Rowan was part of the discussion – something Quinn was thankful for – but Quinn could sense her agitation and was uneasy.

"What happened?" Quinn asked as soon as they were away from the rest of the group.

"Rowan saw an omen in one of the photographs she took of Andrea," Nick replied. "I thought it best to get everyone out of the water so we could consider our options."

Quinn's mouth dropped open. "Um ... what do you mean about an omen?"

Nick lobbed a sympathetic look in his direction. "I love that you're protective of Rowan. You need to work on your poker face, though. That was horrible."

"He knows what I can do," Rowan supplied sheepishly. "He says I could do it when I was a kid. I don't really remember doing it for the first time until I was a little older – until it was my mother – but I've purposely blocked a lot of that out."

Quinn instinctively stroked the back of Rowan's head to offer solace. "It's okay. You can tell anyone you want. It's your secret, after all."

Rowan shrugged. "It's weird. Until today, I thought you were the only other person who knew."

"Well, since he already knew, it's not a big deal." Quinn pressed a kiss to Rowan's forehead while locking eyes with Nick. Something deep passed between them – warning, gratefulness, worry – but they both kept brave faces for her benefit. "So Andrea has the mark. We need to figure out why."

"Perhaps the dive itself is a threat," Nick suggested. "Maybe we should check her equipment or something."

"I'm not above checking her equipment, but we'll have to do it under the guise of checking everyone's equipment or it will look hinky," Quinn said. "As for equipment failure itself, that would be my natural assumption except ... ."

"Except what?" Nick prodded.

"Except that this is the second time it's happened on this trip," Rowan supplied. "It happened with Selena, too."

"And that's why you were watching her so closely," Nick mused. "I wondered if it was something like that. You seemed disturbed that day on the deck."

"Selena is part of Andrea's elite diving team," Quinn noted. "She had the mark. We saved her. Now Andrea has the mark. That can't be a coincidence."

"No, I would agree." Nick moved his eyes to the diving team at the end of the dock. The bulk of the participants were complaining ... and in very loud fashion. "I guess we have to ask ourselves what Selena and Andrea have in common."

"They're both elite divers," Rowan volunteered. "Maybe someone is worried they're going to see something at the wreck, something that someone wants to hide."

"Hmm." Nick pursed his lips. "That's definitely a possibility."

"What could it be, though?" Quinn challenged. "The Conqueror has been down there for centuries. Whatever our guilty party is trying to hide couldn't possibly be anything other than new."

"Unless he or she is looking for something old," Rowan pointed out. "Think about it. What's supposed to be down there?"

"A shipwreck," Quinn answered without hesitation.

"You're being too literal," Nick offered. "I understand what Rowan is saying. We talked about it a bit during the descent, in fact. There's money down there."

"Old money," Quinn said. "It's not as if the coins can be collected, cleaned, and used to buy a new car or something. An antique dealer or coin collector would recognize old Portuguese coins and given the notoriety this find has gotten, it would be very hard to pass them off as anything other than stolen goods."

"That's true," Nick agreed. "The coins are considered historic. Their value goes above and beyond that which they can be sold for if you're dealing with the right buyer."

"Oh." Realization dawned on Quinn as he ran his hand over Rowan's back. "You think there's a turncoat in our midst."

"Wait ... how did you get there?" Rowan was completely flummoxed. "How did you get from a specialized dealer to a traitor?"

"It's fairly simple," Nick replied. "Whoever has targeted the divers did it for a purpose. What's the purpose? It has to be the coins. Even a handful of them could make someone very rich.

"The thing is, we have security procedures in place to make sure no one pockets any of the loot," he continued. "All the divers were divided into set pairs and all collection bags have to be logged once the divers hit the docks. We have third parties waiting right at the spot where the divers exit the water to take possession."

"I still don't understand," Rowan pressed. "How does that lead to a traitor?"

"What's the best way to circumvent the security, Ro?" Quinn asked.

"I don't know. Um ... maybe joining forces with another diver."

"Uh-huh. How do you circumvent the third and fourth parties on the docks watching everything?"

Rowan shrugged. "I have no idea. This is your world. I'm just visiting ... and hoping for an extended leave pass."

"Cute." Quinn poked her stomach. "You circumvent it by having a group of people work together."

"And then you increase your portion of the pie by eliminating members of the group," Nick added.

Rowan's eyes widened to saucer-like proportions. "You're saying that several of the divers are working together."

"And possibly murdering together," Nick confirmed.

"That means if Selena and Andrea were targeted, then they're probably involved," Quinn said. "They'll know who is in charge of this, who is calling the shots."

"Wouldn't that be the buyer who wants the coins?" Rowan asked.

"Not necessarily," Nick replied. "It's far more likely that they'll want to get the coins before they approach a buyer. Bringing a buyer in too early would mean another person to control should things get out of hand. No one thief worth his or her salt would risk that."

"It has to be a man," Rowan said. "It was clearly a man who attacked Selena on The Bounding Storm the other day."

"It could be more than one person, though," Quinn pointed out. "We have no idea who is and isn't involved."

"And that could very well leave us outnumbered," Nick added.

Quinn tightened his grip on Rowan's waist. "I want you to go back to the ship, Ro. I think that's the safest place for you. Nick and I will handle this."

Rowan immediately started shaking her head. "There's no way that's going to happen."

"Oh, it's going to happen," Quinn argued. "You're not safe here."

"Neither are you. You can't go diving with those people again. You're the odd man out."

"I have no choice but to dive with them again. I'm the only one who can figure out what they're doing underwater."

"Not the only one." Rowan pulled away from him, her expression fiery. "I can help underwater. I'll be in the submersible with Nick. I can watch your back for you."

Quinn didn't want to smile. It would only encourage her, after all. He couldn't help himself, though. "I wouldn't want anyone else watching my back. Still, it's not safe for you to stay here. We have no way of knowing who our enemies are."

Rowan was adamant. "I'm not leaving you here."

"Ro ... ."

"It's not going to happen." A muscle worked in Rowan's jaw as she stared him down. "You can't bully me into changing my mind. Don't even try."

Despite the surreal situation, Nick was amused as he watched Rowan stand her ground. "Oh, she's a firecracker. I'm so glad I didn't miss this."

Quinn murdered him with a look. "She's ... something all right. I still don't want her involved in this."

"She'll be in the submersible," Nick pointed out. "There's actually no safer place for her."

Quinn remained unconvinced. "The Bounding Storm is safer. Our people are there."

"You're my people ... er, person," Rowan corrected. "I'm not leaving you."

Quinn turned to stone for a full ten seconds, finally letting loose with a heavy sigh. "Fine. You'd better be careful, though."

"The same goes for you."

"The same goes for all of us," Nick corrected. "Now, I suggest we take a long, hard look at the people over there while we eat lunch. We know what we're dealing with now, if not who. We should be able to figure something out if we all put our heads together."

"Great." Rowan flashed a smile. "Order something good for lunch. I'm starving."

"Only you could be hungry in the middle of all this," Quinn said.

"I'll take that as a compliment."

"I'm fairly certain I meant it to be exactly that."

QUINN KEPT ROWAN close as they settled at one end of a picnic table. There were three grouped together, and he purposely picked the one with the best view to use as his perch.

Nick went the easy route and ordered sandwiches and chips. He also arranged for a supply of juice and water to be delivered. He sat across from Quinn and Rowan and kept the conversation going while watching the divers for hints of mischief.

"So, about the cannon ... ."

"I think it's easy enough to bring up," Anthony said. "We'll take inflatables down, slide them under the cannon and then inflate them so it naturally lifts through the water without being jarring. The depth is not so deep that we have to worry about that."

"No, but I do think there are going to be issues when the cannon hits oxygen," Andrea noted. "It's been under there for a very long time. Only the metal is still intact and it's going to be a mess to clean up. I'm worried that there will be an oxidation effect when we get it to the surface."

"I see." Nick steepled his fingers, giving the approximation of a man in deep thought. "Perhaps we should wait until tomorrow to deal with the cannon. I want to place a call to the home office tonight and see what they have to say. I would hate to ruin the cannon because we moved too fast."

"I think that's a good idea," Anthony said. "Right now we can focus on the ocean floor. I was hoping to get some underwater metal detectors down there to make things easier. Currently we're using the screens and shuffling dirt into them. That's slow going."

"We have that equipment on The Bounding Storm, right?"

Anthony nodded. "I can send a team back to retrieve it."

"We can let that wait until tomorrow," Nick said. "For today, keep on as you're currently doing. Just because the work is slow, that doesn't mean we aren't getting anywhere."

Anthony scowled, obviously unhappy. "Yes, but wouldn't it be better for everyone if we could work faster?"

"Faster is not always better." Nick was firm. "Keep the afternoon shift the way you've been doing it. I will contact the home office and see what they think about the plan to bring up the cannon. We'll talk after dinner. Perhaps tomorrow we will have an entirely new game plan."

Anthony made a grunting sound in the back of his throat as he shook his head. "Fine. You're the boss."

"I am." Nick turned his attention to Andrea. "What did you find this morning?"

"What looks to be a few more coins," Andrea replied. "There were only a handful of them ... five I think, to be exact. We also found a weird disc thing. I'm not sure what it is. It might have something to do with The Conqueror, but it might be something else completely. We won't know until later."

"Keep me informed. I would hope we can make additional progress this afternoon. Given the pace we're working, it seems likely we'll have to leave a team behind and call in for reinforcements when The Bounding Storm heads back to her home base."

"And when is that?" Anthony asked.

"Five days," Quinn answered. "Our company only allowed for the booking because we had a hole in our schedule ... some conference or something fell through. In seven days we leave on another cruise that's already booked. We need the time between now and then to ready for another group of passengers."

"So there's no hope of keeping you guys here longer?" Selena asked, her eyes moving over Quinn's impressive shoulders. "That's kind of a bummer."

Rowan shifted on her seat, uncomfortable. "I'm pretty sure we have to stick to our schedule."

"We definitely do," Quinn agreed, patting her knee under the table as he worked to keep himself from laughing at her response. "I'm not sure what your company had in mind when it planned this thing ... but that's the timetable we have to work with."

"I don't think they thought that far into the future," Nick said. "I believe the only thing they were worried about was getting a team out here promptly. They were very quick when hiring divers, restoration experts, and security."

He conveniently left out the part about that haste possibly

causing them to face some murderous blowback, but that was on purpose.

"I'm sure it will work out," Rowan offered helpfully.

Nick offered her a kind smile. "I'm sure it will, too. Don't fret. Everything will work out how it should."

The group lapsed into uncomfortable silence for a moment, everyone lost in their own little world. There seemed to be a certain amount of bitterness emanating from the table – from Anthony in particular – but it never got a chance to get a foothold because something else happened to shift everyone's attention.

"What's that?" Selena stood, brushing off her hands on her wetsuit before pointing down the way to where a bevy of lights flashed and a group of people stood. The lights belonged to police cars, and there seemed to be a lot of activity about a quarter of a mile down the beach.

"It doesn't look good, does it?" Anthony followed her gaze.

"Perhaps we should check it out," Nick suggested.

"It's not our problem," Anthony argued. "We should get back in the water. We only have limited time to get this job done. That's the priority, right?"

"It is," Nick confirmed. "I still want to check it out."

"We'll go with you." Quinn used a napkin to wipe the corners of his mouth before grabbing Rowan's hand. "I want to see what it is, too."

A handful of people joined them for the walk, including Anthony, even though he clearly wasn't happy about the delay. Selena and Andrea walked ahead of everyone, their heads bent together. Quinn watched them with a studied eye, although they didn't seem to be acting out of sorts.

When the group reached the beach, Quinn squeezed Rowan's hand before moving forward for a better look. He was almost sorry he did when he realized what the island's rescue team was doing. They were retrieving a body from the shallows.

"Son of a ... ." He glanced over his shoulder and searched faces until he found Anthony's. The man looked as shocked as Quinn felt. "Is that who I think it is?"

Anthony didn't answer. He was too lost in the scene playing out as the large body – because the man was truly huge – was dragged from the ocean.

"That's Stuart Dombrowski," Andrea said, her face draining of color as she stared.

"The missing guy from your team?" Nick asked.

Andrea nodded. "I guess he wasn't out having a good time after all."

"I guess not." Nick exchanged a weighted look with Quinn. "Well, this isn't good."

That was the understatement of the year as far as Quinn was concerned. This discovery changed everything, and not for the better.

19

NINETEEN

There was no more diving that afternoon.

The death of one of their own – along with the gruesome body discovery – left a pall hanging over the group. Nick insisted they return to The Bounding Storm and regroup. Even Anthony didn't argue.

Once back on the ship, the diving and restoration crews separated for a private meeting. Quinn considered trying to listen in, but he figured that was overstepping his bounds. Instead he followed Rowan to the tiki bar and indulged in iced tea and a private conversation of his own with his girlfriend.

"Are you okay?"

The question caught Rowan off guard. "Is there some reason I shouldn't be?"

Quinn shrugged. "I don't know. You seem ... quiet."

"I'm trying to absorb everything."

"Everything with Nick, or everything with Stuart?"

"Everything everything."

"That sounds like a lot to absorb." Quinn patted her hand before leaning back in his chair. "I don't know what to make of it. I don't suppose you have Stuart in any of your photographs, do you?"

Rowan instantly started shaking her head. "No."

"How can you be sure?"

"I would've remembered him. He was huge – almost as big as Anthony – and he had a mustache straight out of a porn movie. Trust me. I would've remembered him."

It was the absolute worst time and yet Quinn couldn't stop himself from laughing. "You know you didn't shoot him because you would've remembered the pornstache. Is there any wonder why I'm crazy about you?"

Rowan mustered a small smile for Quinn's benefit before sobering. "Things are starting to happen fast now. I don't understand it, but I sense something is about to shift."

"You're intuitive. That doesn't exactly surprise me."

"But?"

"There's no but. You're intuitive. I happen to agree with you. Something *is* about to shift."

"I don't suppose you know what that is, do you?"

"No." Quinn rolled his neck and stared at the sky for a beat. "I want you to stay on The Bounding Storm tomorrow."

Rowan immediately balked. "We've already talked about this."

"We have," Quinn confirmed, bobbing his head. "I would like to finish that discussion now."

"We finished it at the dock."

"No, we didn't."

"Yes, we did."

"No."

"Yes."

Rowan made a frustrated sound in the back of her throat. "When are you going to realize that simply saying 'no' to me isn't going to make me fall in line and do what you want me to do? You're not my boss."

"Technically I am," Quinn reminded her. "You have to listen to what I say."

"That's not how a relationship works."

Quinn was testy, the afternoon heat and body discovery combining to make his fuse short, but he managed to bite back a scathing retort. Instead of yelling and screaming, he adopted a pragmatic approach. "Where you're concerned, I'm two things. I'm your boyfriend and your boss."

"That sounds like a dangerous combination."

Quinn narrowed his eyes. "Are you threatening to break up with me if I exert control as your boss?"

Rowan realized how her prior statement sounded and tamped down a surge of guilt. "No. I would never say that. I'm sorry if it sounded that way."

Quinn didn't relax despite the denial. "Rowan, just because you're my girlfriend, that doesn't mean I can give you whatever you want."

"I'm well aware of that."

"And yet ... ."

"And yet you're not shutting me out." Rowan was firm as she held up a hand to quiet whatever argument Quinn was about to mount. "You need me."

"I *do* need you. I need you to be alive."

"Who says I won't be?"

"It doesn't matter how you approach this. I want to keep you safe. That means you're not returning to the dive site tomorrow."

"You can't do that," Rowan protested. "You can't shut me out. It's not fair."

"Life isn't fair."

"You sound like my father." Rowan crossed her arms over her chest and flicked her eyes to the rolling ocean. "He used to say nonsense like that."

Quinn refused to rise to the bait and engage in a full-on screaming match. "I'm sure it didn't feel like nonsense to him."

"Whatever." Rowan was bitter. "I can't believe you're shutting me out of this."

"Ro ... ."

"Don't."

"Look at me." Quinn's voice was firm and Rowan had no choice but to lock gazes with him. "I am not doing this to punish you. I'm not trying to be a mother hen. I'm not even trying to be your boss.

"I don't get off on the power when it comes to you," he continued. "You have to see that I'm not doing this simply because I want to control you. I'm doing this because it's the best thing for you."

"And what about you?"

Quinn's eyebrows winged up. "What about me?"

"Who is going to look out for you if I'm not there?"

Quinn's expression softened, although only marginally. "I can take care of myself."

"I know that but ... you need me."

"Of course I do. I can't let you put yourself in danger, though. You have to understand that."

"I'm not sure I do."

"Honey ... ."

"Don't." Rowan held up her hand, defeated. "You're going to do what you want. What I want doesn't matter."

"Don't say that." Quinn knew she was trying to manipulate him into giving in, but he held firm. "You'll be safer here."

"And you'll be on your own."

"I know what I'm doing."

"I guess that means you don't think I do, huh?" Rowan's eyes flashed with annoyance. "Whatever. You win. I'll be stuck here for the day while you're out saving the world. I hope you're happy."

Quinn was pretty far from happy as he watched her turn on her heel and stalk toward the doorway that led to the employee main hallway. "I'm sorry."

"No, you're not."

"Rowan … ." Quinn felt helpless, but he was resolved to keep her on the ship. "You'll thank me for this one day."

"No, I won't."

QUINN EXPECTED ROWAN TO shut him out of her quarters. He thought there was a very good chance they would argue further in the privacy of her room, so he was understandably surprised when he found her already in bed, her face turned to the wall.

"Do you want me to go?"

The question startled Rowan. "Go where?"

"Away."

Rowan rolled so she could see his conflicted face. "What do you mean? You want to go away from me … for good?"

"No." Quinn immediately started shaking his head. "I never want that. I meant for tonight. You're obviously upset. Do you want me to go back to my room?"

Rowan opened her mouth to answer but snapped it shut before she could say anything stupid and make things worse.

"Is that a yes or no?" Quinn prodded.

"I don't want you to leave," Rowan said finally. "I want to sleep next to you. The thing is, I'm still angry."

"Does that mean you're going to go Hulk on me in your sleep? If so, I could get behind that if your clothes rip with your temper."

Rowan rolled her eyes. "Ha, ha."

"I thought that was kind of funny."

"You would."

Quinn sat at the end of the bed and pulled off his shirt. "I promise it's going to be okay. I'll be careful."

"Your promise isn't going to mean much to me if something happens tomorrow," Rowan pointed out. "Just so you know, I'll spend the rest of my life blaming myself if that happens and I'll never get over your death."

"Way to ease the pressure there, Ro," Quinn said dryly as he removed his shorts. He hit the light switch on the wall before crawling into bed. Her body was warm, but she didn't immediately reach for him like she normally did. It was a small tear in the heart. "I won't let anything happen to me. I promise."

"I'm not sure you can keep that promise."

"I'll do the very best that I can."

"Whatever." Rowan's voice was full of weariness, but she rolled to rest her head on his shoulder all the same. "I'm still angry."

"Hulk mad," Quinn intoned.

"I'm going to smash you if you're not careful," Rowan warned.

"If that's the game you want to play."

It took Rowan a moment to realize what he was inferring. "You're a total pervert."

"You say that like it's a bad thing."

"Yeah, yeah, yeah."

ROWAN STOOD NEXT **TO** the gangway that led to the dock and watched Quinn double-check his pack the next morning. She wasn't any happier about the situation than she had been the night before, but she refused to send Quinn off with a scowl – especially because she believed he was walking into danger.

"You have your phone, right? In case you need me, I'll keep my phone close."

Quinn chuckled, genuinely amused. "I have it with me, but it's not as if I can use it underwater. I'm fine, though." He pressed a kiss to her forehead. "Stay close to Sally and Demarcus today. Treat it as a day of rest. You know ... hang out, drink iced tea, and be merry."

"Ha, ha." Rowan cracked her neck. "Try not to be gone longer than you have to. I don't want to worry but ... ."

"I'll be back before you know it."

Rowan didn't believe that for a second. "Be safe."

"You be safe, too." Quinn pressed a soft kiss to her mouth. "It's going to be okay. Believe it or not, I know what I'm doing."

"I do believe it," Rowan acknowledged. "I also believe you're outnumbered."

"I don't think they're all involved. That wouldn't make sense from their standpoint."

"Yeah, but you don't know who is involved," Rowan pointed out. "You simply believe Selena knew something and that's why someone tried to kill her."

"We also know that Stuart Dombrowski was probably involved," Quinn added. "Sure, he could've been killed by a random local, but that's way too coincidental for me to believe."

"Do you know how he died?"

"I've seen the initial medical report. His neck was snapped."

Rowan pictured the huge man on the beach. "That would take a big body to do that sort of damage to a guy that size."

Quinn knew what she was getting at. He'd had the same thought himself. "Baby, I will be back as soon as I can. Don't worry about me."

Rowan stared at him for a long beat. "Just one thing before you go."

"What?" Quinn thought she was going to throw her arms around him, kiss him senseless, and maybe press herself against him so he could have a bit of a thrill before leaving. Instead she lifted the camera he didn't even realize she was carrying and snapped it in his face.

Quinn blinked three times in rapid succession as he tried to clear his head after the surprise flash. "What the ... ?"

Rowan pulled back the camera and studied the photograph in the viewfinder. There was no omen. That made her feel markedly better and yet not free of the pressure building in her chest.

"What's the verdict?" Nick asked, approaching from the south side of the boat.

"What verdict?" Quinn questioned, confused.

"She took the photo to make sure you weren't in imminent danger," Nick noted. "I take it that means you convinced her to stay on the ship."

"Ordered," Rowan corrected. "He ordered me to stay on the ship. He's technically my boss and apparently he can do that."

Instead of sympathizing with Rowan, which she expected, Nick barked out a laugh. "That's one way to defuse an argument."

"I didn't manage to defuse the argument," Quinn countered. "We've agreed to table it until I get back."

"I'm simply glad she'll be here where I can keep an eye on her," Nick said. "I was worried about her hanging at the dock all day."

"You're staying here?" Despite himself, Quinn was relieved. "That means you'll be around to watch her."

"I don't need a babysitter," Rowan grumbled.

"Shh. I'm talking to your uncle." Quinn slid his arm around Rowan's waist to placate her and focused on Nick. "I thought for sure you would be heading to the dive site."

"So did I, but I'm waiting for a visit from the local constable and he suggested meeting here," Nick explained. "I can't really stand him up, so I won't be heading to the site until this afternoon."

"So you'll be close to Rowan." Quinn bobbed his head in approval. "That's good. That makes me worry less."

"You don't have to worry about me," Rowan challenged. "I'm not the one in danger. You are."

"You just took a photo of me," Quinn pointed out. "I didn't have the omen on me, did I?"

"No."

"That means I'm safe."

"That means you're not going to drop dead in the next five minutes," Rowan corrected. "That hardly means you're safe."

"And here we go." Quinn ran his hand over the top of his hair. "Rowan, I know what I'm doing. I know how to take care of myself. We've been over this."

"That doesn't mean I'm suddenly not going to worry," Rowan fired back.

Sensing a potential fight – and knowing neither of them really wanted to engage in it – Nick put his hand to Rowan's forearm to still her. "You'll both worry. You'll both be fine. In fact ... Rowan, why don't you take a photo of yourself and show it to Quinn. That way he'll see you're perfectly safe, too."

Quinn lifted his chin. "Does it work if you take a photo of yourself?"

Rowan shrugged. "I've never tried."

"Do it now."

Rather than argue, Rowan did as instructed. When she pulled back to study the viewfinder, she frowned at the photo. "Ugh."

"What? Do you see it?" Quinn was on the verge of panicking.

Rowan shook her head. "I hate the angle. I look like I have a double chin."

Quinn stared at the photo over her shoulder and swore under his breath. "You look beautiful. In fact, I want a copy of that photo for my desk in my office."

"You're just saying that to make me feel better."

"I'm saying that because it's true." Quinn planted another kiss on Rowan's mouth when he heard footsteps on the deck. He didn't have to look to know that Anthony was approaching. The big man had a certain presence that couldn't be denied. "I'll be in contact. I'll call during lunch to make you feel better."

Rowan nodded solemnly as Anthony clapped a big hand to Quinn's back.

"Are you ready to go, buddy?"

Quinn spared Anthony a look. "I am. Although ... where is Andrea?"

"She already left for the site," Anthony replied. "She's upset about missing the afternoon session yesterday. She wants to make up time today."

"Then I guess we'd better do that." Quinn started down the gangway, casting one final look in Rowan's direction as he increased the distance between them. He blew her a kiss before he hit the dock, lifting his hand in a wave that said "sooner" rather than "later."

Rowan returned the wave with a sigh.

"He'll be fine," Nick said. "You took his photo yourself."

"He'd better be." Rowan knew Quinn wanted her to relax, but she couldn't bring herself to do it. Instead she did the opposite and paced. There was nothing else she could do with her pent-up energy, after all. She was forced to wait. That didn't mean she would do it quietly.

NICK WATCHED ROWAN WALK a groove in the deck from his spot in the shade. For the first twenty minutes after Quinn's departure, he tried to talk her down. That didn't work – not even a little – so he ultimately gave up and drank his juice in the shade while flipping through some expense reports.

Even though he had a job to do, and he genuinely enjoyed doing it, he found he couldn't focus on work when Rowan was such an emotional mess.

"My dear, you're going to make yourself sick if you don't sit down. Perhaps you should join me in the shade."

"I don't want to sit."

"Quinn won't like it when I tell him you spent the entire day fretting about him," Nick noted. "It will make him angry and cause him grief. Do you want to do that?"

Rowan quit pacing long enough to cock a challenging eyebrow. "Are you threatening to tattle on me?"

Nick balked. "Of course not. I just ... was trying to make you sit down. I see now that was a bad idea."

"It certainly was," Rowan agreed, shuffling forward and snagging her camera from the table. She hit the power button and shifted the photos in the viewfinder until she found the one of Quinn. He was still omen free. "He's okay."

"Of course he's okay," Nick said. "He knows exactly what he's doing. He's a strong man. He'll come back to you."

"I hope so."

They lapsed into comfortable silence for a moment, and when

Nick broke it, what he said was enough to steal the oxygen from Rowan's lungs.

"You have no idea how proud of you your father is. He worried about you for so long I thought it might eventually kill him. You've found yourself, though. You're okay. That will be a load off his shoulders."

Rowan turned deathly still as she lifted her chin, her finger inadvertently hitting the "advance" button and landing on the photo she took of herself. "What did you say?"

Nick realized exactly what he uttered when it was too late to take it back. It was obviously a mistake, but that genie couldn't go back in the bottle. "Oh, well ... ." He shifted on his chair, uncomfortable.

"Did you just say my father is alive?" Rowan was beside herself. "You said you had no idea where he was. Were you lying?"

"I ... ."

Rowan licked her lips, her eyes landing on the photo of herself in the viewfinder at the same moment a shadow approached from her left. Rowan registered two things in quick succession. The first was that her photo showed the symbol. It had popped up out of nowhere. The second was that the shadow was raising an arm and there was something off about the figure.

Rowan made out the distinct outline of a gun at the same time she dropped her camera to the table and threw herself on top of Nick, tackling her uncle to the opposite side of the chair and cringing as the gun went off in unison with the "thud" that echoed as they hit the ground.

It seemed things were about to get dangerous, and despite Rowan's worries, Quinn wasn't the intended target.

She was ... again.

20

TWENTY

Nick hit the ground hard, a full-body gasp rocking him.

"What the ... ?"

Rowan couldn't answer because she had other things to worry about, an incoming enemy flooding her internal danger sensors. She spun, keeping low, and surveyed the deck as she tried to find a way to escape. Unfortunately, they were out in the open and there was essentially no place to hide.

"Don't even think about it." Andrea's voice was even as she leveled the gun on Rowan.

From her spot on the ground – which seemed to make her especially vulnerable – Rowan narrowed her eyes and glared at the diving guru. "I can't say I'm surprised you're involved, but I didn't even doubt Anthony when he said you were already at the docks. Kudos to you on your plan. I wasn't expecting it to go down like this."

Anthony. Rowan's imagination sparked with possibilities as she thought of Quinn. She knew almost from the beginning that Anthony had been involved – there was honestly no doubt in her mind – but having it confirmed was another thing entirely. Quinn was with a killer. A big killer, mind you, and there was nothing Rowan could do to warn him.

"Oh, please," Andrea scoffed. "You had no idea I was involved in anything."

"That's where you're wrong." Nick straightened, his gaze busy as it bounced between the tense women. Rowan could practically see him thinking. She just hoped he didn't make matters worse with whatever plan he came up with. "We knew you were involved yesterday. Our only problem was deciding who your partners were."

"Excuse me?" Andrea arched a challenging eyebrow.

"Your partners," Nick repeated. "We knew Selena was one and Stuart Dombrowski the other. We also knew you needed at least one more."

"Anthony," Rowan supplied. "He's the only one big enough to snap Stuart's neck."

Andrea balked. "You don't know what you're talking about. In fact ... I ... how did you even know that?"

It should've been a triumphant moment – other than the gun, of course – but Rowan couldn't shake the feeling that she was still in trouble. She flicked her eyes to the camera on the table and focused on her face. The selfie she took was still visible through the viewfinder and the omen remained.

"We know more than you think," Nick replied, resting his hands on his knees as he regarded Andrea with cool calculation. "You guys should've done a better job trusting one another. Once members of your team started getting attacked, we realized what was happening."

Andrea snorted derisively, although her eyes were alive with worry. "You're making that up."

"I'm not." Nick was unbelievably calm, something that impressed Rowan to no end. "I forwarded your names to the home office last night. They were intrigued and agreed to send another team to clean up your mess."

Rowan was impressed. If Nick was telling the truth, he was even smarter than everyone believed. If he was lying, he was good at it.

"You contacted the home office?" Andrea was flummoxed. "But ... why?"

"Why do you think?" Nick refused to back down. "Andrea, my dear, you may be a good diver but you're a lousy liar. What happened to Selena on the deck was enough to put everyone on edge. It was also enough to have everyone looking at you ... and not in a way that was conducive to your plan."

Rowan rolled her neck as she listened to Nick talk to Andrea, the final pieces of the puzzle sliding into place. She decided to play a hunch. "You shouldn't have killed Stuart so fast after he attacked Selena."

Andrea flicked her eyes to Rowan. "What do you mean?"

"Stuart was the one who attacked Selena," Rowan supplied. "Whatever your plan – or reasons for why you did things a certain way – that was a dumb move. To kill him so quickly after the event ... it simply made you guys look even guiltier."

"You have no idea what you're talking about," Andrea snapped. "We have everything under control."

"You really don't." Rowan adopted a pragmatic tone, as if she were talking to a child and the subject of a timeout arose. Rowan knew it was a risky move, but she had to appeal to Andrea's rational side – if that still existed – because Quinn was out there and in danger. Even though Rowan knew she was in an iffy position, she couldn't stop her mind from traveling to Quinn. Her heart hurt when she thought about him being attacked with no one to help him. "You're out of time and reinforcements are coming. You'll be in custody by noon."

Nick stared at his niece for a long beat, something unsaid passing between them. "Quite right, Rowan," he said. "It will definitely be before noon."

Andrea's eyes lit with something dangerous, but she managed to refrain from melting down ... although just barely. "Oh, well, that's just great! I told Anthony this was a bad idea and we should do it a different way. He refused to listen, though. Apparently he never listens. I knew it and I'm going to scream 'I told you so' in his stupid face the next time I see him."

"How long have you guys been planning this?" Rowan asked, buying time.

"Since we both got hired," Andrea replied. "We weren't lying about only meeting each other on this job. We'd heard about each other, of course. You can't be in this business and not hear about each other. He approached me, though, when he realized what we were dealing with. We made plans before we even hit the ship.

"I honestly wasn't sure if I wanted to throw in with him," she continued. "He seemed like a decent enough guy, but I was wary. He has quite the reputation in certain circles."

"That obviously didn't stop you," Nick noted. "You joined together with Selena. Anthony brought Stuart along for the ride. How many other people were on your team?"

"Just the four of us. We didn't want things to get unwieldy. The bigger your team, the more chances for mistakes."

"You had plenty of mistakes with only four of you," Rowan pointed out. "Why did Stuart go after Selena so early into the trip. Why not wait until later?"

"It was a power struggle," Andrea explained. "Anthony was used to being in charge. So was I. We were trying to make things work ... and yet they didn't. We couldn't agree on anything. That includes a timetable, a seller, and an escape plan."

"That doesn't surprise me," Nick said. "You both have strong personalities."

"We do," Andrea agreed. "We thought that meant we would be dedicated to getting the job done in a quick and efficient way. That hasn't worked out so well."

"No, I'm starting to see that," Rowan said dryly. "Why did you and Selena keep working on this project after what happened? You had to know that was Anthony and Stuart trying to increase their haul when Selena almost went over the railing."

"We had our suspicions," Andrea corrected. "We thought it was probably Anthony and Stuart, but we had no way of knowing. Selena was terrified. She wanted to quit right there. We had the better map of the undersea terrain, though. We thought they needed us.

"I figured that was what Stuart was after when he attacked," she continued. "I thought it was a little too convenient that Anthony chased the assailant and happened to lose him. That was a little too ... fantastical. He denied it, of course, but I knew better."

"You have a map of the terrain?" Rowan scratched the side of her nose. "How did you manage that?"

"Selena's uncle works for the Woodhaven Oceanographic Institute. They have updated maps and they're not available to the public. That was an edge for us when we were searching. It allowed us to plan ahead and we knew exactly what we were looking for when we landed."

"So what was the plan?" Nick challenged. "The four of you were going to work together, hand over a few coins here and there so you could look as if you were doing your job, and then run off with the rest of it. How were you going to make it happen?"

"It wasn't hard," Andrea replied. "We've been collecting stuff since the first dive. We simply don't bring it out of the water. We plan to go back for it when we can and treat it ourselves."

Nick flicked a weighted look to Rowan, but she had no idea what he was trying to say to her.

"I see," Nick said. "You were keeping it under the cannon, weren't you?"

Andrea widened her eyes. "How did you know that?"

"Yeah, how *did* you know that?" Rowan asked.

"The home office looked at the data we sent and said they couldn't understand why Anthony was dragging his feet raising the cannon after he'd been keen to do it earlier, ultimately changing his mind out of the blue. It looked like a standard job to them."

"I told him that would come back to bite him, but he didn't believe you were smart enough to realize it," Andrea said. "I guess I was right on that one."

"I'm guessing that was another problem between you," Rowan said. "You both wanted to be right."

"Anthony's biggest problem is that he wants to be right, but I am always right," Andrea corrected. "It's been something of a ... struggle."

"And it won't get any better," Rowan said. "How do you see this working out? Anthony killed his own guy to cover up what he tried to do to Selena. Do you think he won't do that to you?"

"There's no way he would be dumb enough to go after me," Andrea countered. "After he failed the first time, he pulled back. He knows I'm on to him. He's afraid of me."

Rowan almost felt sorry for the woman. "You're wrong. He was going to kill you yesterday. That's why Nick called off the search before lunch. We were trying to figure out a way to save your life."

Andrea balked. "That's ridiculous."

"And yet it's true," Nick supplied. "Anthony isn't going to stop until you're dead. Well, you and Selena. He wants to be the only one who can claim those coins. Let me guess, he said he killed Stuart because his man went rogue and Anthony had no idea he was going to turn on you. Am I close?"

Andrea was flustered. "But ... he wouldn't do that."

"Oh, he would do that," Nick argued. "That's been his plan from the beginning. Your biggest mistake was not seeing it from the start. I believe you knew better, Andrea." He made a clucking sound with his tongue. "What will you do once we're gone and nothing is standing in Anthony's way?"

Realization washed over Andrea's face. "He is un-freaking-believable. I can't believe this happened!"

Rowan couldn't believe it either. That didn't stop her from glancing at her watch. They were running out of time.

THE DOCK WAS EMPTY WHEN QUINN and Anthony showed up. Quinn knew why. He didn't even have to consider it. From the moment that Anthony met him on The Bounding Storm's deck, Quinn recognized the big security honcho was going to make a move ... and sooner rather than later. Quinn simply had no idea how bold the move was going to be.

"I wonder where everyone is," Anthony mused, making a good show of searching the water for signs of his crew.

Quinn knew better ... and he was done messing around. "I think they're wherever you sent them. You don't have to keep up the act."

Anthony didn't immediately turn to Quinn. He wasn't worried about him, of course. He didn't consider him a threat. Instead, his lips curved, and he kept his eyes on the water. "I wondered if you would figure it out."

"I figured it out long before you wondered if I would." Quinn's voice was grim. "Trust me. You're not as smart as you think you are."

Something in Quinn's voice forced Anthony to shift his head in the man's direction, the move slow and deliberate. He widened his eyes when he saw the weapon in Quinn's hand. He hadn't even considered it when they left The Bounding Storm – he thought Quinn merely wanted the shark spear to protect himself, after all – but now he realized the truth.

He also realized he was at a distinct disadvantage, which was something he didn't expect.

Anthony licked his lips, nervous. "You wouldn't stab an unarmed man with a shark spear, would you? That hardly seems fair."

"I don't care about being fair." Quinn was unbelievably calm. He'd been expecting this all along. He simply didn't want the fight to come in front of Rowan because he knew she might freak out and he didn't want to worry her. He also didn't want Anthony getting his hands on her so he could use the feisty woman who had stolen Quinn's heart as a shield. "I'm not going to be baited into doing something to your benefit, so you can stop talking right now."

Anthony made a face. "I knew you were going to be trouble. I told Andrea and she thought I was crazy. I knew your reputation, though."

"Yes, well, I guess you were right."

"I *was* right." Anthony bobbed his head. "That's why I made sure to have backup on this one. That's the reason I sent Andrea after your girlfriend in the first place."

Quinn's heart did a slow, cold roll. "What?"

"That's right." Anthony warmed to his topic, amused. "Andrea is going after your girlfriend right now. Did you really think I didn't plan all of this out?"

Quinn refused to let his panic show even though his heart rate had picked up a notch. "That's exactly what I think. In fact ... now I know it."

Anthony licked his lips as he darted another glance to the shark spear. "I won't go down quietly. I don't care that you have that. I refuse to lose."

Quinn's eyes darkened. "I was hoping you would say that."

"I DON'T WANT **TO** do this," Andrea offered, her expression rueful. "I don't want to hurt anyone. I wanted to become a thief, not a murderer. Anthony forced my hand. I truly am sorry about this."

Rowan swallowed hard. She knew she was running perilously close to losing everything. Given her position on the deck, though, she had no idea what to do about it.

"If you kill us, which you're probably capable of doing, you'll be playing right into Anthony's hands," Nick pointed out. "We're your last hope for powerful allies. Anthony is out there right now taking care of Quinn. He'll come for you next."

Rowan snapped her head in Nick's direction, furious. "Don't you ever say that! Quinn is fine."

Nick's expression didn't change. "You've seen Anthony. You know he's not going to go down no matter how Quinn fights. Quinn is strong, but he simply can't take Anthony. We need more men to do it." Nick licked his lips, his demeanor utterly calm. "He'll come after you next, Andrea. I can see you know that. You're going to need help if you expect to survive."

Andrea shook her head. "He wouldn't go after me. He's not that stupid."

"You're the stupid one," Rowan hissed. "You're the one here when he's out there planning exactly how he's going to kill you."

"He wouldn't do that."

"He *is* doing that," Nick said. "He's out there plotting your demise. He's probably already got a plan in place to claim the items you've pilfered and disappear from the area within the hour. He'll either kill you or leave you behind. I'm guessing killing you will be the easiest route, though."

"No." Andrea was beyond upset. "He won't. He said he wouldn't do that."

"Yes, and he always keeps his word, doesn't he?" Nick challenged dryly.

"But ... ." Andrea was lost in thought. Rowan thought there was a distinct chance Nick was getting through to her. She didn't have a chance to sit around and watch, though.

"Oh, screw this." Rowan rolled to her back and slammed the soles of her feet into Andrea's knees with as much force as she could muster, catching the stunning diver off guard and causing her to buckle.

Rowan was ready. She caught the gun before Andrea could drop it and slid backward once she did, keeping her eyes on Andrea as she hopped to a standing position. Rowan was on her feet, the gun pointed at the woman who previously held it, before Andrea grunted out a groan of pain and lifted her chin.

"What are you doing?" Andrea gritted out.

"Well, for starters, I'm going to shoot you if you move," Rowan replied calmly. "I'm done playing around with you people."

"Rowan, perhaps you should give me the gun," Nick suggested. He was standing, too, getting to his feet when he realized Rowan was on the attack. "You don't want to accidentally shoot someone, my dear. That's probably not how you want to spend your day."

Rowan snorted. "Don't worry. I know what I'm doing. This is hardly the first time I've been in a situation like this."

"Sadly, I'm starting to believe that's true," Nick murmured.

Rowan's eyes were ice as they locked with Andrea's. "You should've surrendered. We would've taken it into account when we turned you over to the police. Now we just want you to suffer."

"You can't keep me," Andrea argued. "You don't have the strength to hold a gun on me and take me into custody. You're not strong enough to do both."

"I guess it's good that's not necessary, huh?" Rowan said, a small smile playing at the corner of her lips when the security guards who had been grouping in the nearby alcove – the one behind Andrea that she couldn't see – pounded to the deck. "As I said, I have everything under control."

"No!" Andrea fought the first set of hands that landed on her, but it was a fruitless effort.

Rowan took another step back and saluted Demarcus. He'd seen the whole thing go down, ducking behind his bar before Andrea could realize he was there. He'd called for security right away ... and waited. Rowan may have secured the gun, but Demarcus was the real hero.

"You did well," Nick offered, impressed.

"Yeah, we'll talk about that and other things as soon as I find Quinn." Rowan turned so she could head toward the gangway. All she could think about was getting to Quinn, saving him. She had no idea how she was going to do it, but she figured the gun could only help. She didn't get that far, though, because Quinn – his cheek bruised and his brow sweaty – stood in front of her, his chest heaving due to his haste to get back to The Bounding Storm and a lopsided grin on his face. "You're okay."

"That was going to be my opening line." Quinn held out his hand for the gun. "Can I have that?"

Rowan nodded, mute.

"Thank you." Quinn flicked the safety on the gun and placed it on a nearby table. "Aren't you going to say something?"

Rowan worked her mouth, no sound coming out. Finally, she found her voice. Even she was shocked by what came out. "I was just on my way to rescue you."

"Oh, I'm kind of sorry I missed that." Quinn grinned. "I couldn't wait for you. I had to go after Anthony myself."

"But ... how? He's huge."

"Why do you think I took the shark spear?"

Rowan's mind traveled back to the weapon Quinn nonchalantly claimed before leaving The Bounding Storm and felt her insides relax. "You just wanted to get him away so I wouldn't see the fight."

Quinn nodded. "Pretty much."

"That was smart."

"I'm a smart guy."

"Uh-huh." Rowan swiped at a tear on her cheek. "I kind of want to hug you."

"That's good." Quinn sobered. "I definitely need that right now."

"Okay." Rowan threw her arms around Quinn and burst into tears. The emotion didn't surprise him. He'd been expecting it. If his men weren't busy securing Andrea and making arrangements to transport Anthony to the brig, he would consider crying himself.

Instead, he stroked the back of her head and met Nick's studied gaze. "I guess we worked well as a team this go around, huh?"

Nick nodded without hesitation. "We certainly did."

"We had to start somewhere," Quinn mused, swaying back and forth. "Everything worked out. Everything is okay. It could've been worse."

"It wasn't."

"Let's hope it never is."

21

TWENTY-ONE

Saying goodbye wasn't easy. It especially wasn't easy for Rowan the next morning when she realized Nick was staying on El Demonio and an American law enforcement team was traveling there to take Selena, Andrea, and Anthony into custody.

"We haven't had a chance to talk." Rowan was morose as she stood on the dock next to The Bounding Storm. They were set to leave within the next thirty minutes and she was desperate to get answers out of Nick before that happened. "You were busy with everything else yesterday and ... we haven't had a chance to talk."

Nick's expression was sympathetic. "We'll have time."

"But ... ."

Quinn rested his hand on Rowan's shoulder. He sensed her distress but there was very little he could do about it. Rowan filled him on what Nick said right before Andrea's attack and he was curious. He was also resigned to leaving without the answers Rowan so desperately needed. He could see no way around it.

"Ro, we have to leave." Quinn's voice was gentle. "We should already be on the ship."

Rowan ignored him. "Nick ... ."

"Sweetheart, I promise we'll talk." Nick was firm. "This has turned into something of an international incident, though. Our bid on the site is being restructured. We might lose it completely. I have no choice but to focus on what happened here. I promise I'll be in touch on the other stuff as soon as I can swing it."

"What's going to happen with that?" Quinn rubbed his hand over Rowan's back, hating how tense she was.

"Andrea, Anthony, and Selena are all facing numerous charges and will spend time in jail," Nick replied without hesitation. "Selena will be offered a deal if she turns on the other two. She was the minor player in this so it only seems fair. If Andrea and Anthony ever see freedom again, I will be stunned."

"That's what I figured."

"I want to know why you said what you said," Rowan pressed. "I need to know. I ... you can't just leave."

Nick licked his lips as he regarded his niece. "I don't know what you want me to say."

Rowan refused to let it go. Now that she was out of immediate danger – now that everyone was safe – she could focus on nothing but what Nick said to her. She didn't sleep at all the previous night, instead tossing and turning as she struggled with the endless possibilities that flooded her mind. "Where is he? Is he alive? You referred to him in the present tense."

"I can't talk about this here." Nick cast a glance over his shoulder and nodded to the local constable when the man gestured for him to approach. "I really have to go. You do, too."

"But ... ."

"I'm sorry." Nick meant it. He stepped forward and grabbed Rowan's shoulders, tugging her in for a tight hug before she could mount further argument. "I swear I'll be in touch just as soon as I can. We'll make arrangements to meet in Florida."

"Just tell me," Rowan implored, her eyes filling with tears. "You have to tell me something."

Nick opened his mouth, conflict evident on his face. Finally, he leaned as close as he could and whispered. "He's alive. I can't tell you more than that. I will when I can ... but now is not the time. You don't understand what's happening.

"I am so sorry for putting this added strain on you," he continued. "You can never know how sorry I am. I hope to be able to alleviate it soon, but I can't do it now. It's simply impossible."

Nick pulled away, his eyes glassy. He stared at Rowan long and hard, but she didn't utter a single word. She couldn't. She was too stunned.

Because he knew they were short on time, Nick turned his full attention to Quinn. "Take care of my niece. She's going to need you now more than ever."

Quinn pursed his lips. "What you've done here is cruel."

"It wasn't my intention."

"That seems to be your mantra." Quinn slipped his arm around Rowan's waist. She didn't fight the effort, but she didn't melt into him either. "I'm completely pissed off that you've done this to her."

"And I don't blame you." Nick held up a finger to still the constable. The man was getting antsy, and with good reason. American authorities were due to land within the hour and Nick was spending the bulk of his time trying to placate his niece. "I am sorry. There are a multitude of reasons for my secrecy, and I can't go into them here."

"Then you never should have said it," Quinn snapped.

"It wasn't my intention to say it. The words slipped out. I thought we would have a chance to discuss things ... but that's clearly not the case."

"Clearly," Quinn said dryly, gripping Rowan tighter to his side. "If you don't get in contact with her, I swear to you, I will hunt you down. You won't like what I do when it happens either."

"I believe you mean that." Nick stroked his hand over the top of Rowan's head. "I really have to go." He brushed a kiss against Rowan's forehead. "You'll be okay. I'll be in touch. That's the best I can offer you right now."

Rowan was stiff when she stepped back, her eyes dark and furious. "You have a job to do. You'd better do it."

Nick's stomach twisted at her lost expression. "I will be in touch as soon as I can. Believe me, I'm sorry."

"Whatever." Rowan turned on her heel and stepped on the gangway. It took everything she had to put one foot in front of the other and leave behind the answers she'd been seeking for a decade. Her anger was overwhelming, but there was nothing she could do about it so she merely kept walking.

Quinn waited until they were on deck to speak again, worry practically overwhelming him. "I'm sorry this happened, Ro, but he was very obviously in a spot. He couldn't tell you what you needed to hear. It was a confluence of things that no one could've seen coming."

"That seems like a convenient excuse," Rowan argued. "He could've told me before all this happened. He had plenty of time then."

Quinn swallowed hard. "The last thing I want to do is take Nick's side."

"Then don't."

"I don't see where I have a lot of choice." Quinn offered up a sheepish smile. "He wanted to get to know you before he dropped that bomb. He wanted to see how you would take it. He thought he had more time."

"I can't believe you're standing up for him." Rowan was flummoxed. "That's the last thing I expected."

"I'm not standing up for him," Quinn clarified. "I'm standing *with* you. There's a difference."

"I don't see how."

"Whatever he has to tell you, it's big." Quinn kept his voice low as he glanced around to make sure no one was listening. "He doesn't want to do it in front of other people. He also doesn't want to do it when he doesn't have enough time. He said he'll be in touch."

"Do you believe him?"

Quinn tilted his head to the side, considering. "Yes," he replied after a beat. "He wouldn't have come here if he didn't want to fix this. I believe that's exactly what he wants to do."

"He lied, though," Rowan pressed. "He said at first that he had no idea what happened to my father. That's clearly not true."

"And I also think it's clear that whatever he's hiding is something that can't simply be spread around with little thought to how it's going to hurt everyone involved," Quinn said. "He'll tell us more when he can. I have faith in that. You should, too."

"But ... ." Rowan looked so helpless Quinn could do nothing but tug her to him.

"It's going to be okay," Quinn whispered, swaying back and forth as he tried to offer comfort. "I think you're going to get the answers you need. It's not going to happen today – and that's what you want – but it is going to happen."

"So I'm just supposed to wait?"

Quinn nodded. "I know it's hard but there's nothing else I can do."

"Well, this sucks."

Her lament caused Quinn to smirk. "It definitely sucks."

"What am I supposed to do until I get my answers? I'm going to drive myself mad while I'm waiting."

"It's funny you should mention that." Quinn offered up a mischievous grin as he pulled his head back and stared into Rowan's soulful eyes. "I believe there's a Jacuzzi I've been dying to show you and I can guarantee no one will be in it for the ride back to Florida. It's ours for the taking ... for the next two days."

Rowan didn't want to encourage him – it seemed somehow wrong, after all – but she couldn't stop herself. She brightened considerably. "That's the best offer I've had all week."

"I was hoping you would say that." Quinn pressed a kiss to her lips. "We'll figure it all out. We can't do anything right now, though, so we might as well take some time for ourselves."

Rowan heaved out a sigh. "Okay, but I'm going to expect a massage when we're in this magical Jacuzzi."

This time Quinn's grin was so wide it practically took over his entire face. "Finally something I want to do."

"Yeah ... that goes for both of us."

Made in the USA
Monee, IL
26 June 2020